Drawings by Jason Rosenstock

Amulet Books
New York

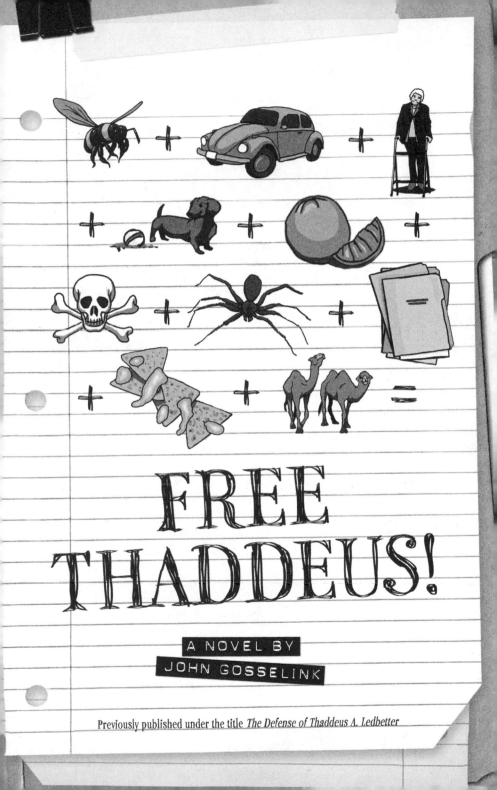

FREE THADDEUS!

A NOVEL BY
JOHN GOSSELINK

Previously published under the title *The Defense of Thaddeus A. Ledbetter*

The Library of Congress has cataloged the hardcover edition of this book as follows:

Gosselink, John.
The defense of Thaddeus A. Ledbetter / John Gosselink.
p. cm.
Summary: Twelve-year-old Thaddeus A. Ledbetter, who considers it a duty to share his knowledge and talent with others, refutes each of the charges which have sent him to "In-School Suspension" for the remainder of seventh grade.
ISBN 978-0-8109-8977-1
[1. Conduct of life—Fiction. 2. Middle schools—Fiction. 3. Schools—Fiction.
4. Student suspension—Fiction. 5. Humorous stories.] I. Title.
PZ7.G688Def 2010
[Fic]—dc22
2009052209

Paperback ISBN: 978-1-4197-0084-2

THE ART OF BOOKS SINCE 1949
115 West 18th Street
New York, NY 10011
www.abramsbooks.com

To my
sweet wife,
Ally

IN-SCHOOL
SUSPENSION

Discipline Referral Form

Student's Name: Thaddeus Ledbetter ___ Grade: 7 Gender: M

Teacher's Name: _____

Location of Offense: CCMS _____

Reason(s) for Referral

_____

"The True Emergency Drill"

_____

_____

Previous Corrective Action(s) Taken by Teacher

- ☒ Student Conference _____ Times
- ☒ Time-Out/Loss of Privilege
- ☒ Seating Change
- ☒ Phone Conference with Parent
- ☒ Face-to-Face Conference with Parent
- ☐ Other _____
- ☒ Referred to Counselor
- ☐ Behavior Contract
- ☒ Letter Sent Home

Action(s) Taken by Administrator

- ☐ Discussion
- ☐ Warning/Probation
- ☐ Student Conference
- ☐ Contacted Parent
- ☐ Detention
- ☐ D.A.E.P. Assignment
- ☐ Other _____
- ☐ Verbal Reprimand
- ☐ Referred to Counselor
- ☐ Detention
- ☒ In-School Suspension (ISS)
- ☐ Expulsion
- ☐ Referral to Law Enforcement

Administrator Signature Principal Frank Cooper _____

Student Signature Thaddeus A. Ledbetter (soon to be Esq.) _____

Crooked Creek Middle School
Morning Announcement Request

Please include the following announcement:

February 2

Mr. Cooper, please announce that today's scheduled meeting of the American Society of Fun Facts has been canceled because the club's president is stuck in In-School Suspension (thanks a lot).

Maybe you should also warn the student body that they can actually get In-School Suspension for the rest of the year even if they do NOTHING wrong!

Since we're on the subject, I've been meaning to mention to you, on a stylistic note, that maybe you should do the announcements in rhymed couplets. Something like:

> If you are feeling tough and a bit macho
>
> You'll enjoy today's lunch of a delicious nacho

This might help kids pay attention more. When you drone on and on over the intercom every morning ("Blah, blah, blah, progress reports . . . blah, blah, blah, don't chew gum"), everyone just kind of zones out after a while. So when you get to the important announcements, no one hears them.

Your poor presentation also hurts attendance at my club meetings.

Sincerely,

Thaddeus A. Ledbetter (soon to be Esq.)

Crooked Creek Middle School

5

Student: <u>Thaddeus Ledbetter</u>   ID number: <u>2234</u>   Birth date: <u>8/16</u>

<u>1/11</u> Thaddeus performed his own safety drill at our school today involving a pest control team, classic cars, and many natural-disaster drills. When I asked how he thought this could be a good idea, he claimed it was a "True Emergency Drill." Due to these drills, the school was overrun by local news trucks, and coverage reached a national level. Between the Dunham lawsuit, the Citrus League threatening litigation, the church fire, and complaints from the art coalition, this is the last straw.

<u>1/12</u> We had a discipline hearing this morning concerning all of Thaddeus's recent and numerous discipline matters. Several people voiced their complaints. Many feel Thaddeus has become dangerous to himself, the other students, and the community at large. As a result, I have decided to remove him from the general population and have assigned him to In-School Suspension for the rest of the year. I truly believe this is the best thing for everyone involved. While these drastic measures are unprecedented, I feel Thaddeus's offenses warrant unprecedented actions.

(In retrospect, when Mr. Nelson, Thaddeus's elementary school principal, sent me a note wishing me "good luck," I probably should have seen this coming.)

<u>1/15</u> Thaddeus began his ISS in the portable building behind the bus barn (yet he still had time to draw up another one of his "school improvement plans"). I'll add it to the others.

Dog holding pen—currently space used for encyclopedias. We haven't used hardcover encyclopedias in this millennium.

Students having easy access to their dogs increases their ability to learn.

Dog snack storage area

Side note: this is an excellent time to seriously consider smaller class sizes. Not only is it better for learning, but we could fit a lot more dogs.

FRANK COOPER, *Principal*

Thaddeus,

I'm placing you in In-School Suspension for the rest of the year. Here is a map to your assigned room (it's not on the official map, so I drew it in). You are to go directly to your room and NOT have any contact with students or teachers.

Mr. Cooper

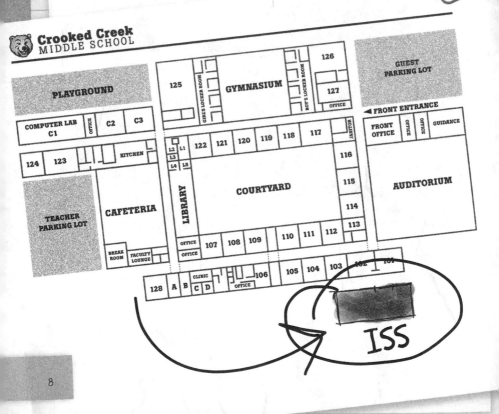

THADDEUS A. LEDBETTER
DEFENSE

To: Mr. Cooper, Principal of Crooked Creek Middle School

From: Thaddeus A. Ledbetter, student

Subject: To have Mr. Cooper reconsider his decision to put me in In-School Suspension for the rest of the year. REST OF THE YEAR?! My uncle Pete didn't think it was possible to be in In-School Suspension for the entire year. He even started laughing when I told him last night. My mom used to say Uncle Pete was a bad influence (he's my dad's younger brother), even though (or maybe because) he's a lawyer. But he says she just needs to lighten up. Or at least, he used to tell her that.

(I know technically I was supplied this laptop to do all of my schoolwork electronically, but I think that using it to write my defense against this failure of justice is more important. I'm sure you'll agree after reading it. And in the interest of full disclosure, I will include all pertinent correspondence, notes, and other materials. If you, Mr. Cooper, were a true man of honor, you would also supply me with any exculpatory evidence that might help with my defense. See Fun Fact for explanation.)

A Thaddeus Fun Fact
"Exculpatory" means evidence that proves the accused (me) is innocent. There is also "inculpatory" evidence, which proves guilt. (But there is none of that kind of evidence in my case.)

DEFENSE

Mr. Cooper,

Please consider this a formal protest in response to the meeting on Tuesday. I mean, c'mon! Having all those people in one room together with their complaints, yelling, and finger-pointing, it was pretty much an ambush. I figured you wanted to talk to me about the True Emergency Drill when I was called to the office, but I was surprised to walk into a meeting of an angry, agitated mob of adults. (Look, I just naturally used alliteration, a device useful in poetry and the blues. That's pretty impressive.)

Furthermore, your decision to isolate me for the rest of the school year is very extreme. Basically, you are removing the heart and soul (and especially the brain) of the entire student body. It makes no sense. Are you trying to impress other principals or something? "Oh, other principals give a kid two weeks' detention? Big deal, I'm so tough that I put Crooked Creek's most important student in ISS for the entire year!" There's better ways to impress people.

Thaddeus Fun Facts

A close study of literature, comic books, and spy movies indicates that isolating highly intelligent people leads to the emergence of criminal masterminds and mad supervillains who can cause great damage to the world. Just something to think about.

• • •

Alliteration is the use of the same consonant sound at the beginning of several words close together, as in "principals pick poor punishments for productive prodigies." Or "disaster drills designate dire dilemmas for dummies." I've got more if you still don't understand.

THADDEUS A. LEDBETTER
DEFENSE

And I especially don't appreciate the "outstanding members of the community" giving you a standing ovation when you announced I was going to be locked away for the rest of the year. Was that really necessary? If these people are so outstanding, don't they have something better to do than celebrate the injustice carried out against one kid?

Hey Uncle Pete,

Just wondering if you have had time to look at my case. I think litigation may be needed. You say you like to fight for the little guy, and I'm real little. Just twelve, and a little over five feet tall.

Oh, and when my mom got mad because you were laughing at me getting In-School Suspension for the rest of the year, I think she was just transferring her anger about my situation onto you. But I guess angry is better than sad, so in a weird way, it was kind of a nice change.

So if I need to give a supposition or something, you know where to find me.

Your favorite nephew (and also your only one),
Thaddeus

Thaddy My Boy,

I haven't had the chance to look at your case, but from what your mom has said, I think you may just want to accept your punishment and learn from this experience.

If there are legal charges brought against you (please tell me your little episode wasn't the one I saw on the news where the entire emergency rescue department had to evacuate a school), I will definitely represent you. But let's just hope this suspension thing is the worst of it.

Yes, you are my favorite nephew, but why don't you just cool it for a while? Your mom is having a tough time with everything and doesn't need this. Remember, you promised to use your tools of efficiency and preparation for the common good.

Uncle Pete

How is preparing the school for the worst possible emergency not a good deed? How come none of you adults are getting this? Geesh. My dad would have understood.

Thaddeus,

Whatz up, Dawg . . . How's jail treating you? (LOL) I'm sitting in Mrs. Garza's class and I am sooooooooo bored. Guess what: we're having another notebook checkbbb

This is like the millionth time. What's the deal with this teacher and notebooks? Kind of weird.

Did you see our school on the news? When those policemen with the helmets and masks were running around and yelling I was soooo scared. I know you were involved in some way since you are in school jail, but what's the whole story? I've been telling people it was Billy Cunningham's fault (I saw him pull the fire alarm), yet you're the one being blamed because some of the teachers don't like you.   (over)

14

Well, got to go turn in my notebook. Hope you get out soon.

Oh, and my mom wanted to thank you for the thank-you note for the flowers we sent to the funeral. That's a lot of thanking. She hopes you are doing OK.

Oh yeah. I'm having some kids over Saturday to watch some movies. You're invited.

Check ya later ;)
Alison

P.S. Hope you get this. Mrs. Wilkes said she would deliver my notes when she brings you lunch. I think she misses you and all your compliments on her nachos.

15

Thaddeus,

I don't think you understand how much trouble you are in. Young man, I would advise you to get your schoolwork done. Please try to keep your comments about my job performance to yourself. I've been a principal longer than you've been alive, so I think I know what I'm doing, and I'm not interested in your school-improvement plans.

Mr. Cooper

Crooked Creek Cafeteria

Thaddeus, are you sure you want nachos EVERY DAY for lunch? We're having sloppy joes and chicken nuggets this week. I can slip you another fruit cup if you want. Nachos every day is not very nutritious.

Mrs. Wilkes

POSSIBLE THADDEUS FUN FACTS:

* Look up "sinister." I think it has something to do with being left-handed. Maybe look up some of the bad people in history and see if they were left-handed. Maybe Hitler was. I wonder what hand Mr. Cooper uses.

* I wonder if anyone has studied what kind of damage a hummingbird the size of a turkey would do. It would have to eat at least twenty pounds of nectar a day to meet its metabolic needs. That's a lot of begonias.

* Check American Sign Language dictionary to see what the sign for "toaster" is. I bet motioning "popping-up" is involved.

* Humans are defined as "mammals" from the Latin "mamma," meaning "producing milk." Since only the females of our species produce milk, are the males actually "mammals"? Hmmm, maybe I could coin a new word . . . how about "Thammalians" for men?

* Someone told me that people doing yoga repeat the same, boring noise constantly to help them concentrate on nothing. I need to look this up because if it is true, Mr. Cooper's droning announcements may take yoga to a new level of concentration.

DEFENSE

Notwithstanding the lack of maturity by the supposed "adults" at the discipline hearing, the biggest error you made was not allowing me to defend myself. Sure, if you listen to all of those angry adults, it does sound like I cause a lot of trouble.

But instead of forcing me to sit there quietly and be yelled at, if you allowed me to explain the mitigating circumstances ("mitigating" is a lawyer word for reasons why things are not as bad as they seem. I'm not sure if they covered that in your principal training), I think you would find that not only should you not be punishing me, you should be rewarding me, probably with a public ceremony and a plaque. If a plaque isn't affordable, I'll accept a certificate suitable for framing. (See below.)

CROOKED CREEK
MIDDLE SCHOOL

Certificate of Overall Excellence
Presented to
THADDEUS A. LEDBETTER

In recognition of the outstanding contributions he has made to the community, Crooked Creek Middle School, and the world. We are all better people for having been around such a thoughtful and prepared young man.

Not only that, but I wanted to remind you what a valuable asset I am to this school and this community. In fact, it's really the school that's being punished by not having me around. Mr. Cooper, just think of the numerous ideas I put in the suggestion box outside your office every week and how they could help the school. Let's face it, you need me.

About these ideas, obviously your team is still in the planning stage of implementing my school improvement suggestions. If you could fast-track the "important-student lane" idea, you'll see a significant productivity increase across the campus. I've attached another copy of how to engineer it, with revisions to the initial submission. This is pretty straightforward, but if you'd like me to do a presentation for you, I'd be happy to.

CROOKED CREEK MIDDLE SCHOOL

Please note that the new (and may I say superior) logo for Crooked Creek I designed is a registered trademark ® by Thaddeus A. Ledbetter, Inc.

Thaddeus,

Rest assured that I have read all of the items that you have put in the suggestion box. When I tell the student body I value their input, I mean it.

However, as for your suggestion for an "important-student lane," there are many problems:

1) Who and what determines who the "important" students are? I have a feeling you would volunteer for such an assignment, but we like to think all of our students here at Crooked Creek are important.

2) How would we enforce such a rule? I really don't think the teachers would care for "important-student lane" duty.

3) How do students cross the hall to get to their next class? I don't want tardiness to increase because students are unable to step across three feet to get to their classroom.

While I appreciate your concern, maybe we should focus on getting your grades up and keeping you out of trouble.

Thanks,
Mr. Cooper

View of the 100 Hall of Crooked Creek

THADDEUS A. LEDBETTER
Résumé

If my "important-student lane" isn't enough evidence of what I can offer this school, I would like to highlight some of the other ways I try to better the school. This could take all day, so I am just going to highlight some of the major bullet points on my résumé.

For entire résumé, please visit thaddeus-ledbetter.com

- **Honor roll student** (though not always reflected in reports based on the old-fashioned and out-of-date grading system of A, B, C, D, and F. What a horrible system. Why do you determine someone's academic success by assigning arbitrary letters based purely on how they fall alphabetically? Why not use some other meaningless group, like reptiles. "Hey Mom, I made three turtles, a snake, and a crocodile. I think that's good." Instead, my academic success is measured in real-world results and helpful class-improvement suggestions.)
- **Ordained acolyte of Crooked Creek Church** (temporarily suspended). I will be allowed to light candles in the sanctuary again after completing a weeklong workshop next summer on safe candle-lighting techniques. Surprisingly, I am a student and not an instructor, but I agreed to attend so that the church will be able to have me in their congregation again. This might involve the insurance company. We had a slight misunderstanding earlier this year, which you heard about during the discipline hearing, but I'll be back soon.

THADDEUS A. LEDBETTER
Résumé

- **State champion in academic dictionary skills competition**
  (two years running). Though Crooked Creek Middle School
  only competes at the district level, I can confidently say I
  would have won state if they would have let me compete. Have
  you ever asked another seventh-grader what a word means,
  or its etymology? We really need to work on the curriculum.
  These kids aren't learning much. When I get to high school, I
  will finally be able to compete, and win, not only on the state
  level, but the national level. Maybe even global.

- **Very close to being a qualifier for the President's Fitness
  Challenge** (The pull-up test is unreasonably demanding, and
  I have written to the president to explain why it should be
  changed. We're seventh-graders, not U.S. Marines.)

A Thaddeus Fun Fact

The least-used physical movement for humans is pulling oneself up.
Unless you spend a lot of time hanging off cliffs or find yourself in a
lot of Road Runner cartoons, you will perform the pull-up maneuver
approximately three times in your life. (And that's usually to pull yourself
up over a fence to look at a construction site.)

- **Member of 11 groups, clubs, and organizations, including,
  but not limited to** (in some cases, I am the only member, but
  I'm happy to send you an application form, Mr. Cooper):
    - **Boy Scouts of America:** Though I'm in a bit of a rough
      spot right now with the local troop, I'm in good standing
      with the national organization. First Class Rank (will be

Star Rank as soon as Scout Leader Hardy gets his act together on the paperwork and stops wasting all his time with things that don't concern the Scout troop—future Eagle Scout for sure).

- **Friends of the Planet:** I am the youngest member of this group (we meet at the coffee shop that smells kind of funny on Saturday mornings) and I have the shortest hair, but they nod a lot when I'm giving my suggestions, so they have the good sense to value my input.

- **The Chess Club**

- **Arachnid Appreciators of America:** "Arachnid" means "spider," by the way. Spiders are much more interesting than most people think. They do not deserve all of the screaming and smashing that most people do, unless a poisonous spider is about to attack a loved one.

Loxosceles reclusa, more commonly known as the brown recluse. The venom of this spider causes blistering, flesh deterioration, possible need for amputation, and even death!!! That's why, when I thought I spotted one on my mother's shoulder, I took appropriate action and immediately started swatting her with a broom to dislodge it. It was actually a piece of lint. (She could have been more appreciative for the good deed I was trying to do. And there was no need to yell.)

BOY SCOUTS OF AMERICA

★ ★ ★ ★ ★ ★ ★ ★ ★ ★ ★ ★ ★

Thaddeus,

I am writing you to inform you that your membership in the Boy Scouts of America is in extreme jeopardy. Not only were your actions at the Crooked Creek Nursing Home incredibly ill–advised and dangerous, but they also have cast the entire troop in a bad light. Not to mention the blatant disrespect you have shown my aunt Gladys Appelworthy at your tenant meetings.

Remember your oath:
On my honor I will do my best
To do my duty to God and my country
and to obey the Scout Law;
To help other people at all times;
To keep myself physically strong,
mentally awake, and morally straight.

Having heard the reports of some transgressions you have committed, I have ample cause to dismiss you from our organization. If you have anything to say in your defense, I need it before our next Scout meeting.

Scout Leader William Hardy

★ ★ ★ ★ ★ ★ ★ ★ ★ ★ ★ ★

BOY SCOUTS OF AMERICA

★ ★ ★ ★ ★ ★ ★ ★ ★ ★ ★ ★ ★

P.S. Please inform the Citrus League that your "Citrus Kills" campaign is not associated in any way with the Boy Scouts of America. And please tell Principal Cooper that your True Emergency Drill was neither sanctioned nor supported by us either. We condemn both.

★ ★ ★ ★ ★ ★ ★ ★ ★ ★ ★ ★ ★

THADDEUS A. LEDBETTER
Résumé

+ **The Committee to Improve Crooked Creek Middle School, or the CICCMS:** You really should consider this one. After your apprenticeship period, you might earn voting privileges.

+ **The Real World Preparedness Society (True Emergency Drill Coordinator):** Though the Scouts give a lot of lip-service to "Be Prepared," it has been my experience that we spend a lot more time at our Scout meetings making lanyards out of leather strips and having fund-raiser car washes, neither of which prepares you for anything. (What do kids need with lanyards, anyway?) So I have started a group in which the true focus is preparedness. We practice many different types of first-aid, cancer prevention, disaster reaction plans, and drills—one of which you are already familiar with.

+ **The American Society of Interesting and Fun Facts (a.k.a. Thaddeus's Fun Facts):** You may have noticed that I like to pepper my writings with interesting facts, thus the founding of this society. I think it is only right to share my expansive knowledge with the world. Though the society cannot be held responsible for the "accuracy" of its facts, all Fun Facts are the property of the president of this society, Thaddeus A. Ledbetter, and may only be used when paying a fee to him.

THADDEUS A. LEDBETTER
Résumé

- **The Young Etymologists:** In case you don't know, "etymology" means the study of word meanings and histories. This comes from the Greek words *etymos*, meaning "true," and *logos*, meaning "word" (which is an etymology of the word "etymology").

For example, your surname, "Cooper," means "barrel maker," so you must come from a long line of barrel makers. You might want to consider this as a profession—I'm sure someone needs barrels today. I mean no disrespect, but some of your recent decisions as a principal make me wonder if you are really cut out for this line of work.

THADDEUS A. LEDBETTER
Résumé

+ **Competitive Slug Bug League (Commissioner):** This role actually led to some of those people yelling at me at the discipline hearing. Leadership has its sacrifices.
+ **Students with the Blues (the music, not depression and/or mental illness):** I'm almost finished with my latest song, "Why Is Everybody Yelling at Me Blues."
+ **Future Lawyers of America**

Surely, even you, Mr. Cooper, with all of the above evidence, can understand the disservice you are doing to yourself and the student body by placing me in In-School Suspension. It's almost criminal.

And speaking of criminal, I was really offended yesterday with the irresponsible way some of my accusers were throwing around terms like "manslaughter" and "reckless endangerment," and even "blasphemer" in my direction. My work in the Future Lawyers group lets me know that calling someone bad names without evidence is considered libel. Or maybe it's slander. The one where you say lies aloud, not write them down. I'll research this and get back to you.

DEFENSE

A Thaddeus Etymological Fun Fact

The word "blasphemy" comes from the Greek *blasphemia*, meaning "profane speech, slander, or to speak evil of." None of these terms apply to me in the least. If anything, it should be applied to all you adults who have been saying such awful things about me. Maybe Mrs. Appelworthy should know what a word actually means before she starts throwing it around in a public forum.

Anyway, attached you will find detailed, highly researched documentation explaining all of the mitigating circumstances ("mitigating" means . . . Oh, wait, I already explained that to you. Please refer to earlier page of the defense) of my case. They will prove I have done nothing wrong. Yes, even the "True Emergency Drill" that has everyone so worked up and was the proverbial straw that broke the camel's back (and transformed me from "mischievous and incredibly annoying kid" to—what was the phrase?—"hard-core felon"?) can be explained.

A Thaddeus Fun Fact

It would be impossible to break a camel's back by adding a single straw, even if you dropped it from an airplane or blimp, which would be difficult since it wouldn't drop straight down. Plus, when you think about it, maybe we should come up with a metaphor that doesn't involve the crippling of an innocent pack animal. I may bring this up in the next Friends of the Planet meeting.

THE TOP-SECRET PRISON JOURNAL OF THADDEUS A. LEDBETTER

If you're reading this, that means I didn't make it. I'm not real sure what would have happened to me—maybe a bee attack (though I am impervious to spider bites, I seem to be allergic to bee stings) or cancer (it runs in my family)—but something has happened that has allowed someone (that would be you) to get his hands on this journal. You should feel greatly honored, though a bit sad, too. Please make sure it gets passed along to the appropriate historians.

This journal is to document the trials and tribulations during my unfair and unjustified incarceration. In this case, the prison is not a jail cell, but rather the In-School Suspension room behind the bus barn at Crooked Creek Middle School.

Why I'm here is a long story that I really don't feel like going into right now. The point of this journal is to record my thoughts and ideas as I go through this ordeal. And to provide some documentation for future generations.

Plus, it gives me something to do. I am SOOOOOOOO bored already. So, let's get to it.

DAY 1:

- Started secret prison journal. Seems to be going well so far. Mrs. Calhoun, the aide in charge of the long-term ISS prisoner (who happens to be me), spent the day reading the paper and talking on her phone for a long time to someone named Shirley. Shirley seemed to be having digestive problems.

- Listened to the loudspeaker for the announcements and recommendations I submitted to Mr. Cooper. I didn't hear them. Or at least I don't think I did. I kind of zoned out after a while, since he didn't use rhymed couplets. Wondered if he got my submission.
- Had nachos for lunch.

DAY 2:

- Everybody yelled at me to do some schoolwork, so I did some math. I was supposed to find the lowest common denominator. I'm not sure what this has to do with anything. Isn't asking me to find the lowest common denominator sending the wrong message? Using this logic, I'll also try to get the lowest grade I can get on this assignment.
- I'll start paying more attention when we get to learn useful things like how to engineer bridges or how to build space shuttles.
- Started work on a defense against my incarceration. Trying to keep it simple so Mr. Cooper can understand it.
- Nachos for lunch.

DAY 3:

- Continued work on my defense, accentuating how valuable I am to the school and the community. I didn't really realize how impressive my résumé was until I started outlining it for Mr. Cooper.
- Read a story for English about a monkey paw that gives wishes that turn out badly. Why didn't they wish for their wishes to turn out well? Duh.

- Got math homework back. Reached my goal of finding lowest common grade.
- Sounds like Shirley is more regular. Mrs. Calhoun took a two-hour nap.
- Nachos for lunch.

DAY 4:

- Supposed to write a report on a president. I chose William Taft. I remember hearing somewhere that he was so fat, he got stuck in a White House bathtub. I can't find out how they got him out. I doubt they greased him up with butter, since he would have probably eaten it before they could apply it.
- Uncle Pete e-mailed me back. Not sure he is going to help me. Didn't he promise my dad he would look out for me? I'm hoping he comes through for me on this one.
- Nachos for lunch.

DAY 5:

- Finished introduction of my defense. It is so impressive that it could almost stand alone. I also peppered it with Fun Facts to keep people's attention. Maybe if Mr. Cooper learns something while reading it, he'll be more apt to listen to my explanations.
- Didn't get any schoolwork done (a good defense takes a long time).
- Nachos for lunch.
- I was grounded all weekend (that was real boring, too). Alison was having a party, and I was probably needed to hook up the DVD player or something. She's always needing help with

something, and it seems like her mom is always wanting me to fix stuff. How many people have to be hurt, or at least inconvenienced, in the name of punishing me?

DAY 6:

- Got a letter from Scout Leader Hardy. He wanted to talk to me. Maybe I should send him my defense, too. He still seems to think I am a threat to the Scouts. For a guy who works with kids, he only seems to believe adults. If my dad was here to explain things to him, I know the Scout Leader wouldn't be so mean and narrow-minded.

- Sounds like Shirley is having trouble with her hip. Mrs. Calhoun doesn't even pretend she's not sleeping anymore. Even brought a pillow.

- Nachos for lunch.

DAY 7:

- Don't feel like doing anything today. Not really hungry. All of this isolation is starting to get to me. I've rearranged the ISS room four times to be more efficient, and found the coolest place in the room for Mrs. Calhoun to nap. She seemed really appreciative. I've done all I can in here.

- Worked up a list of character witnesses to send to Uncle Pete. Maybe this will get him moving on my case. I knew I should have had a lawyer on retainer.

- I REALLY wish my dad was here.

Hey Uncle Pete,

Not to tell you how to do your job, but I'm thinking some character witnesses might be helpful in the speedy resolution of my case. I've compiled a list of candidates, trying to focus on those who are well spoken. This is harder than you think. Most kids my age like to accentuate their points by punching you in the arm. Here's a list:

Alison Baker: She's real nice, though a bit obsessed with the state of her lip moisture. She must go through a stick of lip balm a day. She also freaks out if she sees a bee. And she says "like" in about 90% of her sentences, but doesn't mind when I correct her and is really cool. I have to go to her house all the time to fix stuff for her mom, so she owes me. Let's put her at the top of the list.

James Roe: He probably feels guilty after what happened during the True Emergency Drill and would want to be helpful. And he is fairly well spoken, though a bit skittish. He likes to hide behind the bleachers in the gym when things get a little hairy.

But he's a fellow Boy Scout, and that should give him credibility. Not to mention there was an ugly incident where he lost his bike, and I think he is still looking for justice.

Kurt Brewsky: He owes me, too. Back in third grade, the teacher was scolding him about eating his paste, and I pointed out that paste is made of flour, so technically he was meeting his daily grain requirements. I'm fairly sure he's stopped eating paste, but we may want to do a background check on that. People don't find paste-eaters credible, and he really needs to brush his teeth more.

Mrs. Wilkes: She's the cafeteria lady in the Mexican food line and always gives me a little extra cheese on my nachos. You may not think her nacho preparation is relevant to my case, but I think it's a good indicator of the quality of her character.

Senator John Allen: I don't actually know the fine representative from our great state, but you've got to figure he would be helpful in my case. Maybe you could make some calls?

There are some people who, because of their character flaws, we want to stay away from. They include:

Billy Cunningham: The day I met him in first grade,

he punched me because I only had one pudding cup and not one for him. In his world I'm supposed to bring an extra pudding cup for a kid I didn't even know existed. He's been punching me daily ever since, not to mention he makes a soap dish seem intelligent.

Mrs. Dixon: She has this HUGE hang-up about her weight. You say one little thing about her rethinking that cinnamon roll she's about to eat and she flips out for an hour. You have no idea what's going to set her off, so I don't think having someone so unpredictable would serve us.

Mr. Kessel: He's actually a cool guy who used to live in my apartment building. He introduced me to the blues with his record collection. But it turns out, as an accountant he was embezzling from that guy who owns all the dry cleaners around town. Not sure which way to go with this one. He knows everything about the blues, but does that whole being-in-prison thing work against him as a character witness? Your call.

Your favorite nephew,
Thaddeus

THE SLUG BUG
INCIDENT

Discipline Referral Form

Student's Name: _Thaddeus Ledbetter_   Grade: _7_ Gender: _M_

Teacher's Name: _____

Location of Offense: _off-site_____

Reason(s) for Referral

He tried to kill me with a bus!!!

Previous Corrective Action(s) Taken by Teacher

- ◻ Student Conference _____ Times
- ☒ Time-Out/Loss of Privilege
- ◻ Seating Change
- ◻ Phone Conference with Parent
- ◻ Face-to-Face Conference with Parent
- ◻ Other _____

- ◻ Referred to Counselor
- ◻ Behavior Contract
- ◻ Letter Sent Home

Action(s) Taken by Administrator

- ◻ Discussion
- ☒ Warning/Probation
- ◻ Student Conference
- ◻ Contacted Parent
- ◻ Detention
- ◻ D.A.E.P. Assignment
- ◻ Other _____

- ◻ Verbal Reprimand
- ◻ Referred to Counselor
- ◻ Detention
- ◻ In-School Suspension (ISS)
- ◻ Expulsion
- ◻ Referral to Law Enforcement

Administrator Signature _Principal Frank Cooper_____

Student Signature _Thaddeus A. Ledbetter (soon to be Esq.)_

THADDEUS A. LEDBETTER
DEFENSE

PERCEIVED DISCIPLINARY ACCUSATION #1:

The verbal and physical assault of Mr. Douglas Dunham

ACTUAL EVENT:

A gross misunderstanding and overreaction by Mr. Dunham,
a.k.a. "The Big Man in the Big Red Shirt"

. . . .

Mr. Cooper, this is an easy one.

First, a little background is needed on this misunderstanding.
It all began during the Slug Bug Competition that took place
during the seventh-grade trip to the Modern Art Museum.

Speaking of which, you know how people look at modern
art and say things like, "My five-year-old could do that"? Well,
they're right. What a scam. Just draw some squigglies, give it an
important-sounding name, say you want to "push the boundaries
of what people consider 'art,'" and watch the suckers' money roll in.

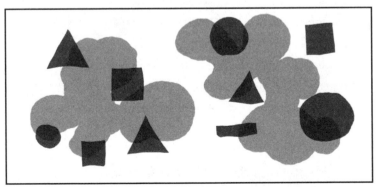

**I call this work *Society Has Killed My Soul* or *My Hamster*—
whichever you prefer. That will be one million dollars, please.**

DEFENSE

Anyway, on the way to this "art" museum, there was a scoring miscalculation during a slug bug competition between Billy Cunningham and me. This caused me to add a special provision to the rules, something I could do since I am chairman of the rules committee as well as the president (see attached rules and regulations as constituted by the Slug Bug Competitors of America).

What happened was this: As usual, Billy Cunningham was my opponent in the slug-bugging. Surprisingly, the skills he has developed as a bully, like being able to determine which sixth-grader has lunch money or who can be an easy victim for extensive noogie-ing and wedgies, and the ability to punch quickly without rhyme or reason, translate into making him good at slug-bugging. With a quick eye, exceptional long-range vision, and a competitive spirit, he is a worthy opponent, though not as good as he thinks he is.

A Thaddeus Fun Fact

It is a good idea to measure yourself against people more talented than you, but you have to be careful not to go too far out of your league or it might do damage to your self-esteem. People with low self-esteem like to punch you for no apparent reason.

Anyway, we were in a tight competition, we both had fourteen points, and we were nearing the museum. The next score was probably going to decide the winner. We were passing one of those popular coffee places (I've noticed that people who drive slug bugs seem to really like coffee) and I was scanning the back of the parking lot when Billy shouts, "Yellow slug bug, no tag-backs, right there in front of the museum! Ha, in your face, Loserhead!!!!"

You have to understand, this was a really big accomplishment. You should have seen his face. No one had ever beaten me before at Slug Bug (at least according to my scoring). There have been a few ties over the years, but no one had actually outscored me mano a mano, or womano a mano for that matter. I post all of the results on my website, thaddeus-ledbetter.com, under "Slug Bug Competition Results," so you can verify this fact for yourself.

I was about to graciously accept my defeat as we approached the museum, even though I don't have a lot of practice at losing, but then I noticed something very interesting. The winning slug bug was not a slug bug at all. More to the point, it wasn't even a vehicle of any sort. It was a sculpture of modern "art." Again, I do use the term "art" loosely. It was a sculpture in front of the museum, that is, if you consider a big rock painted yellow a sculpture.

Slug Bug = Modern "Art"

"Beep-beep!"

"Mmmm, interesting."

(That's what you say when looking at modern art.)

You can see how these could be confused.

Basically, it was a big, round boulder painted yellow. Up close, it was definitely not a slug bug, but from far away, some would argue that it could be easily confused. I, of course, would have never made such a mistake, and was deducting two points from Billy for "slug-bug misidentification" when I was very loudly and aggressively informed that it would not be fair to do so.

See, Billy started shouting that anyone would have made that mistake. He got everyone else all worked up, too, which caused even more unnecessary shouting. You can't imagine the cacophony that can be created when you have a bunch of kids shouting on a bus.

A Thaddeus Fun Fact

"Cacophony" comes from the Greek word *kakos*, meaning "evil, bad," and *phone*, meaning "voice." We can assume that there are a lot of buses full of screaming kids in Greece for this culture to come up with such an appropriate word. It's interesting that the bus driver always starts shouting for everyone to shut up, because that just adds to the noise.

Noticing that popular opinion was against me, and the fact that Billy threatened to punch me in the throat if I tried to take his points, I decided that there should be a special provision for objects that could be reasonably mistaken as slug bugs, though you had to have at least one person agree with you that it was something that could be easily and honestly mistaken for a slug bug.

A Thaddeus Fun Fact

Top 10 things shouted at me at various times, including, but not limited to, field trips and during cacophonies at various locales (many of which I really don't believe I deserve and some I don't understand):

10) "I don't have any idea what you are talking about!"*
9) "Who died and made you boss?"
8) "You'll do anything to win!"
7) "What's that smell?!"
6) "I don't think that's a good idea!"*
5) "I don't care! Get away from me."
4) "Are you crazy?!"
3) "No one wants to know the history of that word."
2) "Thaddeus, give it a rest!"
1) "Why are you so weird?"

*Said repeatedly, and quite unprofessionally, by teachers.

Official Scoring Guide of the Competitive Slug Bug League
CROOKED CREEK CHAPTER
Commissioner Thaddeus A. Ledbetter

OBJECTIVE:

In the game of Slug Bug, the goal is to be the first one to spot a roundish vehicle of a certain make (not named here because of proprietary reasons), announce its color, and "slug" the arm of the closest fellow participant (ceremoniously and without malice).

POINTS & DEDUCTIONS:

If you spot and correctly identify, you will be given the following points:

- Basic color slug bug +1
- Purple +2
- Lime green +2
- Mauve +2
- Multicolored +3
- Pink -2 (unless you're a girl)
- Driver is wearing a cowboy hat +5
- Dog in passenger seat +3
- Dog in driver's seat +10
- Clown driving +3

- 10 or more clowns exit the slug bug +10
- Slug bug upside down +20
- Slug bug broken down on the side of the road -1
- Food/spit comes flying out of mouth while shouting "slug bug" -3
- Milk comes shooting out of nose while shouting "slug bug" +2

In the event of a false slug-bug call,
2 points will be deducted from overall point total.

The "easily confused slug-bug" addendum: If an object is something that could rightfully and easily be confused for a slug bug from a distance, and this opinion can be verified by a non-contestant in the event, no penalty will be deducted.

THESE RULES ARE CORRECT AND ENFORCEABLE AS DETERMINED BY COMMISSIONER THADDEUS A. LEDBETTER, FUTURE ESQUIRE.

Hey Uncle Pete,

I didn't get any notes from you after sending you the
opening statement of my defense, so I assume you like
my changes. I agree.

   I know you're really busy, but if you get a
chance, drop me a line. (That's an old-fashioned
way of saying write me a letter, or e-mail, for the
twenty-first century, though I'm not sure what a line
has to do with writing. Maybe a commentary on poor
handwriting—"just scratch out a line with a few bumps
in it," it seems to be saying.) Anyway, it would be
nice hearing from you. I am sooooo bored.

   Though it has inspired a new blues song: "I'm So
Bored That My Ears Fell Off Blues." (Yes. I am aware
that boredom cannot actually cause body parts to
detach from the body. It's for effect. In the music
biz, this is known as taking artistic liberties. Oh,
and you also get to use bad grammar in blues songs,
about the only time this is appropriate.)

Your nephew,
Thaddeus

I'm So Bored That My Ears Fell Off Blues

(A Blues Song by Thaddeus "Babytooth" Ledbetter)

I ain't done nothing wrong
Yet I always get blamed
They try to bury my talent
And you know that I've been framed

Oooooh, I've got the I'm so bored that my ears fell off blues
Oh mama, them so bored that my ears fell off blues
Yeah, my ears are clattering all over the floor
I think they even got stuck under my shoes
Don't say anything interesting, 'cause I ain't hearing no more

They stuck me in a windowless room without a class
With a lady who likes to nap
I've been accused of having a lot of sass
But they stuck me with a bad rap

Oooooh, I've got the I'm so bored that my ears fell off blues
Oh mama, them so bored that my ears fell off blues
Yeah, my ears are clattering all over the floor
I think they even got stuck under my shoes
Don't say anything interesting, 'cause I ain't hearing no more

(snoring noise as song plays out)

Thaddeus A. Ledbetter

Mrs. Garza

American History

How Historical Quotes Would Have Been Better

Many of the quotes we identify with great people and historical events are poorly written. Maybe with a little planning, or an editor, these quotes could have been better. I've gone through a famous historical quote dictionary and fixed several of them. Maybe you can work these into your curriculum.

1) Franklin Delano Roosevelt could have really made an impact if he had said, "The only thing we have to fear is fear itself, and sharks." Everyone knows sharks are scary, and maybe the fear of shark attacks would have gotten people working hard to get out of the Depression faster.

2) When Neil Armstrong first stepped on the moon, his first words were "That's one small step for man, one giant leap for mankind." I don't even know what that means. Maybe he was drunk. Or had some weird space sickness. Regardless, he should have practiced more. How about, "In your face, Commies!" That would have been cool.

3) John F. Kennedy's famous inauguration challenge should have been, "Ask not what your country can do for you; ask what you can do for your country—like paying your taxes." Maybe this would have gotten all those deadbeats paying their share.

4) Abraham Lincoln started the Gettysburg Address with "Four score and seven years ago." How about keeping it simple with "Eighty-seven years ago"? It's more concise, and the audience isn't asking itself how long a "score" is, or digging for a calculator to do the math. Plus, the speech is so short, folks would have missed it while figuring out the math.

5) Marie Antoinette supposedly said about the peasants, "Let them eat cake." I think this one actually works. Maybe if they were enjoying some delicious cake, the peasants wouldn't have cut her head off.

Thaddeus,

The assignment was to do a report on Dolly Madison, not rewrite the great quotes of history. They've survived well enough without your help. Please write the assigned report.

Mrs. Garza

P.S. I need to check your notebook.

A Thaddeus Fun Fact
(Dental Edition)

Sharks have rows of teeth that move forward to replace those lost in the front—another reason why sharks are scary and superior killing machines. Though it would be cool if humans could move teeth to the front of their mouth instead of wiggling baby teeth out.

It was this special "easily mistaken slug-bug" rule that led to my trouble this year.

The seventh-grade class field trip was to City Hall, apparently for a "civics lesson." You don't realize some of us have spent extensive time at City Hall. I've even spoken several times during the public comments portion of city council meetings, presenting my city planning improvement suggestions, as well as many emergency preparation plans. If it weren't for budget constraints, I'm sure they would have implemented my "hard hats for every citizen in case of meteor shower" program.

Then they passed that "must be a registered voter of this town to address the council" point of protocol, which I have a sneaky suspicion was directed at me, since my ideas were much better than those of most of the council members and it might hurt their reelection chances. If you are interested, I've been looking for a spokesman for my ideas at these meetings.

THADDEUS A. LEDBETTER
DEFENSE

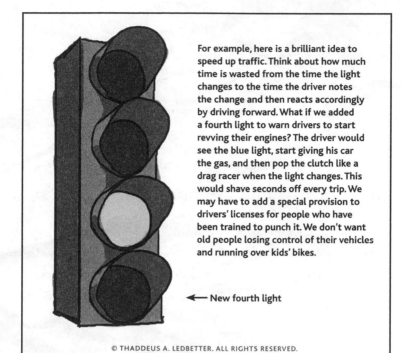

For example, here is a brilliant idea to speed up traffic. Think about how much time is wasted from the time the light changes to the time the driver notes the change and then reacts accordingly by driving forward. What if we added a fourth light to warn drivers to start revving their engines? The driver would see the blue light, start giving his car the gas, and then pop the clutch like a drag racer when the light changes. This would shave seconds off every trip. We may have to add a special provision to drivers' licenses for people who have been trained to punch it. We don't want old people losing control of their vehicles and running over kids' bikes.

⟵ New fourth light

Now that I think about it, this is just as bad as the tenant association at my apartment building giving me only five minutes to make my suggestions. Are you adults just bound and determined to live in an inefficient and unprepared world?

After a thoroughly boring tour of City Hall (during which I swear I saw the mayor change directions when he saw me coming, which is a shame because I had brought along some more ideas for him), we headed back to school.

Crested Ridge Tenant Association Board
Minutes of the Tuesday, October 1 Meeting
Secretary Janice Clemons

8:00 p.m. Meeting brought to order by Association President Terry Petenson, agendas distributed.

8:01 Color swatches for new couches in the lobby reviewed. Board votes to go with mauve.

8:06 Discussion about new drapes tabled until next meeting.

8:07 Tenant comment portion of the meeting.

Mrs. Appelworthy, apartment 714, reports that Dr. Johnson, Thaddeus Ledbetter's dachshund, destroyed the Cuddly Creature stuffed animal collection she had put up on the 7th floor to add a more friendly tone to the building.

Mr. Petenson reminded Mrs. Appelworthy that she was put on the agenda to present her plan to put fake potted ficus plants at the elevator doors on each floor, not to complain about Thaddeus again.

Mrs. Appelworthy produced the decapitated head of "Humphrey the Hippo" and showed bite marks that she claimed were made by a dachshund.

Thaddeus Ledbetter, apartment 710, stated that Mrs. Appelworthy had no training in forensics, let alone canine forensics, and the jury should disregard her statement.

Mr. Petenson said there is no jury and Thaddeus needed to save his comments until his appointed time on the agenda. Board member Fred Dillon excused himself to the bathroom.

Mrs. Appelworthy stated she was just trying to brighten the "mood" of the building with her Cuddly Creatures collection, and asked Thaddeus directly if Dr. Johnson had destroyed her collection.

Thaddeus made the key-locking-the-mouth gesture and pointed at the agenda, indicating he wouldn't talk until his scheduled time. Mrs. Appelworthy threw Humphrey's head at Thaddeus and started crying.

Mr. Dillon returned and informed the board that the meeting room's bathroom was out of toilet paper. Mr. Petenson told him this wasn't the time for that and for Mr. Dillon to deal with it. Mr. Dillon said he had to leave.

Mr. Petenson tried to console Mrs. Appelworthy and gave her a tissue.

Board Member Betty Howard moved that Mr. Dillon could have used those same tissues in the bathroom. Mr. Petenson said enough with the stupid toilet paper already.

Mr. Petenson announced that Mrs. Appelworthy's time was up and Thaddeus would have five minutes to address the board, and he was to limit his comments to his idea of trash chutes for every apartment's kitchen.

Thaddeus said that at this point, he would neither confirm nor deny the involvement of Dr. Johnson in the destruction of the Cuddly Creatures.

Mr. Petenson said to either discuss his trash chute proposal or sit down. He didn't care about any stupid Cuddly Creatures, toilet paper, or anything else and didn't know why he wanted to be president of the Residents Board.

Thaddeus passed out copies of a printout from a website describing the early symptoms of dementia, having highlighted the "excessive and illogical preoccupation with collections and other minutiae."

Mrs. Appelworthy started crying again. Mr. Petenson tried to give her a tissue, but Mrs. Howard had put the box in the bathroom. Mr. Petenson then said some words I prefer not to put in the minutes.

8:39   Board voted unanimously to no longer allow resident comments during board meetings.

8:42   Mr. Petenson closes meeting and sneezes violently. Can't find a tissue, so he uses his sleeve.

DEFENSE

Billy Cunningham was playing well, and we were tied 10–10. We were only ten blocks from school, and I admit, I was desperate. My unbeaten streak was on the line, and I was quickly scanning every specialty coffee shop (there seem to be many these days), used music stores, and other haunts that are favorites of the slug-bug crowd, when about five blocks up the road, at twelve o'clock, the hardest angle to spot for those not in the front seats of the bus, I saw a red slug bug!

"Red slug bug, five blocks up, twelve o'clock, no tag-backs. Billy Cunningham, we are no longer tied!"

A Thaddeus Fun Fact
(Wartime Communication Edition)

Fighter pilots, as well as slug-buggers, use the traditional twelve-hour clock reading as opposed to the military standard twenty-four-hour "hundred" clock, as in "Enemy plane at three o'clock, take evasive measures!" They found that during the afternoon, pilots were impaired in their decision-making when trying to calculate military time. "What?! Plane attacking from eighteen hundred hours? Where is that again? Let's see, subtract twelve hundred and . . . ahh, I'm hit. I'm going down, and I blame this horrible system!"

But again, during the fog caused by intense competition, a mistake was made. The first thing that raised my suspicions that something might be awry was that the slug bug wasn't moving up the road as we approached. That was curious.

Then a way-too-happy Billy shouted, "That's not a red slug bug! That's a fat guy in a red shirt waiting at a bus stop!! Ha, two-point deduction! I win!"

OK, up close it was definitely a fat man. But from far away, and from a moving bus, it was an honest "slug bug" sighting. It was obvious that the "easily mistaken slug-bug" provision was going to go into effect. We were still in a tie, but for some reason, I could not get anyone else on the bus to admit the fact that this particular gentleman could be easily mistaken for a small economy car.

Slug Bug vs. Fat Guy in a Red Shirt

"Beep-beep!"

"I believe I'll have another sandwich."

Again, these are obviously and easily confused.

DEFENSE

Not a single kid on the bus would admit the need for the "mistaken slug-bug" rule, probably out of fear of getting punched by Billy, so I had to take matters into my own hands. With my winning streak at stake, I only had one option that would give me the support I needed to prove this gentleman fell into the "easily mistaken" category.

I went to the source for verification.

As we stopped in front of the bus stop, I pulled down my window and very respectfully asked, "Excuse me, sir, with all due respect, as a man of your girth, are you occasionally mistakenly identified as a subcompact car?"

I said it just like that, saying "with all due respect," and "girth" instead of "fat," and everything. There was absolutely nothing to get worked up about. Still, this guy gets mad—REALLY mad. Like, his face became as red as his shirt and he hops up—well, as fast as a man his size can hop up (it was more of a slow and painful raising of his rather cumbersome and unwieldy frame). Nonetheless, he starts toward the bus.

"Grrrrr, I'm really angry for no apparent reason. I must have problems with being asked very appropriate and respectful questions."

Hey Sexy (in a friend way),

I heard that you were working on getting out of ISS. If anybody can do it, you can. You'll wear down Mr. Cooper and he'll let you out just to shut you up, like you did to Mrs. Taylor in sixth grade to get us a longer recess.

That was sooooooooo cool.

After a couple weeks, I think everyone is starting to miss you, except for maybe the teachers. A teacher will say something dumb and everyone will wait for someone to say something about it, but it's all quiet. I guess we got used to you keeping them in line.

I even heard Billy Cunningham say he wishes you were back so he could punch you in the throat.

If you or your mom need anything, let us know. (I know, you NEVER need help, you give help, but my mom wanted to let you know she's there if you need her. Me, too.)

Peace out,
Alison

Crooked Creek Cafeteria

Thaddeus, your account is running low and I need your mom to send some more money. And yes, I know you want nachos for lunch. You don't have to fill out the order form everyday. We get it—you like nachos.

Mrs. Wilkes

Yo, Dork

If you write me a paper on Dolly Madison I'll give you five bucks. Maybe I won't punch you in your monkey face either. Nah, I'll still punch your monkey face but u can keep the five bucks.

Punch U later, loser
Billy "Slug Bug Champ" Cunningham
(send the paper through your "girlfriend" Alison)

Crooked Creek Library

LATE NOTICE

PATRON: Thaddeus Ledbetter

BOOK: *Famous Quotes from History*

LATE: 4 days

FINE: $.20

Reading Is Power

Well, when the fat man came storming toward the bus, all the kids start freaking out and screaming. Yeah, I didn't get it either. Not sure how many bus trips you have been on, but it takes very little to get a busload of kids freaking out. The driver clips one curb on a turn and you would think someone's head had exploded in the rear seat. I mean, what did they think that fat guy was going to do? Eat the bus?

Then you know how Mr. Hines (the bus driver) doesn't always pay attention? Or maybe you don't know. Mr. Cooper, you really don't keep a finger on the pulse of the school as you should. That's why I am so necessary to help improve things. Speaking of that, I have been working on a questionnaire that you should use when screening possible bus driving candidates. Please see attached.

Prospective School Bus Driver Competency Test

Please indicate on a scale of 1 to 5 (with 1 being "never" and 5 being "always") how often the following statements, actions, or thoughts occur to you:

1. I shout for no apparent reason.   1 2 3 4 5
2. When stopping at train tracks, I take a quick nap.   1 2 3 4 5
3. The sight of schoolchildren makes me think, "I hate them so much!"   1 2 3 4 5
4. If someone suggests I find a "wingman," I want to punch him in the face.   1 2 3 4 5
5. I believe eating nachos on my bus should be a capital crime.   1 2 3 4 5
6. I would let the big kid on the bus enforce discipline with mixed martial arts moves.   1 2 3 4 5
7. If the student is not standing in the exact spot for pickup, even if he is doing something very important at the time, I will not pick him up.   1 2 3 4 5
8. When getting helpful advice from a passenger, I prefer to ignore it and just point at the "Don't Talk to the Driver" sign.   1 2 3 4 5
9. If kids start screaming, my first instinct is to throw the bus in reverse.   1 2 3 4 5
10. I have the urge to hit fat people with my bus.   1 2 3 4 5

If results are 12 points or fewer, give this man a bus license. If score is 13 to 25, possible driver with adequate training. A driver who scores 26 or higher should be let nowhere near a bus and placed in a less demanding job like barrel maker or school principal.

THADDEUS A. LEDBETTER
DEFENSE

Well, I believe Mr. Hines was thinking about something else instead of paying attention to his bus responsibilities when everyone started screaming. He must have thought he had daydreamed through the light change, so his initial reaction was to punch the accelerator, and the bus lurched forward. Luckily, he quickly realized the light hadn't changed and didn't plow us head-on into cross traffic, but he was still in the middle of the intersection with traffic speeding toward us.

So Mr. Hines slams the bus into reverse to get us out of danger. Mind you, everyone is screaming like crazy for various reasons, even Ms. Longoria, and she's usually pretty levelheaded for a teacher. But as the bus quickly backed out of the intersection, the highly emotional fat man in the red shirt (the aforementioned Mr. Dunham) had reached the curb. Disaster at this point was a matter of fate, and who can blame fate on me? (Please see accompanying diagram for this unfortunate, yet unavoidable and definitely not-my-fault series of events.)

Wham-o, Mr. Dunham smacks himself in the head with the bus's rearview mirror, knocking himself unconscious. Someone shouts, "We just killed that fat man!" and the screaming just goes berserk. It was pure pandemonium.

A Thaddeus Fun Fact

The word "pandemonium" comes from the Greek *pan*, meaning "all," and *daimonion*, meaning "demons," as in "making a racket like a lot of demons." Now, I'm not sure exactly how many demons there are; I wonder how you would find out. I'm going to ask Pastor Snodgrass after he calms down about the fire thing. He loves those kinds of questions. But anyway, that's how the bus sounded after the fat guy hit himself with the bus.

THADDEUS A. LEDBETTER
DEFENSE

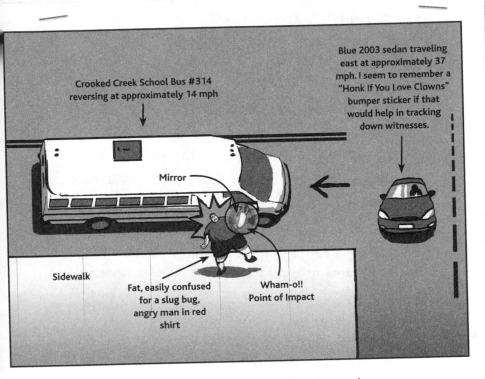

Crooked Creek School Bus #314 reversing at approximately 14 mph

Blue 2003 sedan traveling east at approximately 37 mph. I seem to remember a "Honk If You Love Clowns" bumper sticker if that would help in tracking down witnesses.

Mirror

Sidewalk

Fat, easily confused for a slug bug, angry man in red shirt

Wham-o!! Point of Impact

I seem to remember a dog here, or maybe a man wearing a sombrero. I can't remember.

Luckily, being a highly trained First Class Boy Scout, I knew what to do. While everyone else was screaming, I ran to the front of the bus, opened the door—Mr. Hines was shouting into his radio something about it not being his fault (don't you hate when people don't take responsibility for their actions?)—and commenced performing CPR on Mr. Dunham.

Thaddeus,

I've been contacted by the legal counsel of a
Mr. Douglas Dunham. They informed me that they
are considering both a civil lawsuit as well as
pressing assault-and-battery charges. WHAT THE HECK
HAPPENED?!!!

Boy, it's a good thing you're a minor. This isn't
really my area of expertise, but I'll make some calls.

I'm going to try to make it over for dinner this
weekend. I'm sorry I've had to cancel the last two
times, but things kept coming up. I really do want to
spend some time with you, and I will. We can do some
"man" things, like burping and killing spiders. Oh
wait, I forgot about your love of spiders. We'll do
something else. What did you and your dad always do?
Go to the Natural History Museum? We could do that,
or maybe try out one of your safety drills?

AND PLEASE STAY OUT OF TROUBLE.

Uncle Pete

My Weenie Dog Is Chasing the Devil
(A Blues Song by Thaddeus "Babytooth" Ledbetter)

When I was just a young boy
A couple of years ago
I had me a weenie dog
That could not be controlled

He'd tear up your stuffed animals
Even if you kept them on a high level
He didn't care who owned them
He'd even chew those of the devil

I've got dem weenie dog blues
Oh mama, those weenie dog blues
Let me tell you again in case you
Weren't paying attention
I've got dem weenie dog blues

I'd go and answer the door
And the weenie dog would shoot out
Like lightning he'd flash down a floor
Then eat dem stuffed animals
And cause that old lady to shout

I've got dem weenie dog blues
Oh mama, those weenie dog blues
Let me tell you again in case you
Weren't paying attention
I've got dem weenie dog blues

(make assorted "bow-wow-wow" noises)

67

DEFENSE

> ### A Thaddeus Fun Fact
>
> Besides the Pledge of Allegiance to the United States, kids in Texas are also required to say a pledge to the state of Texas. How weird is that? You can read it online. I guess if South Dakota ever invades Texas, the state government can count on the kids to come to their aid.

Knowing the urgency of the need for some CPR (and having practiced many, many times on my dog in preparation, and wanting to try it out on someone who really needed it), I didn't actually go through the preliminaries of checking for his vital signs, which in retrospect, I now believe might have been a mistake. Mr. Dunham wasn't dead—not even close to it. He was just knocked a little loopy.

So when I leaned toward his mouth to begin reviving him, his eyes flew open and he started screaming. (Again with the screaming! That was the theme of the day!) But instead of being grateful for my concern for his welfare, he's all huffing, and breathing hard, and turning super red—even redder than before, maybe even fuchsia—and screaming right in my face, "Get this hideous kid off me before he kills me or I kill him. I'm gonna sue him and his rotten school." Or something along those lines. He was kind of hard to understand at this point.

(I'm pretty sure I saw a copy of the lawsuit in my official folder. I'm confident the case will be dismissed when I explain what happened. By the way, Mr. Cooper, would you mind if I listed you as a character witness? How's the school's defense, by the way? I'd be happy to help.)

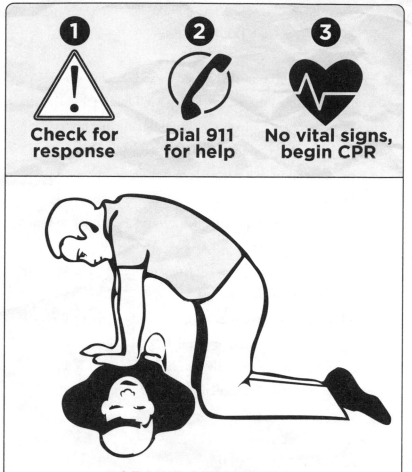

1 Check for response

2 Dial 911 for help

3 No vital signs, begin CPR

ADULT CPR STEPS

Tilt Head.

Give

Administer 30 co

Continue until he

or it is imp

This is what the CPR I was performing looked like, except he was in the red shirt, not me. I believe I was wearing yellow. And he was a lot fatter—I mean, a lot fatter. Like twice as big as this guy.

THADDEUS A. LEDBETTER
DEFENSE

It was about this time that the police and the ambulance showed up and toted the still screaming Mr. Dunham off. I'm not sure where they took him, since he was only suffering from crazy overreaction, a condition the hospital can't really help with.

To sum things up, my alleged crime of verbally and physically assaulting a man borders on the ridiculous. How about politely asking a gentleman an innocent question and then trying to help in his time of dire need?

Again, you should be congratulating me and my quick thinking, *not* locking me away.

(Oh, and I'm sure you're curious—the official ruling I passed down as Slug Bug Commissioner is that Mr. Dunham meets the requirement as something easily confused for a slug bug. The contest ended in a tie. I am still undefeated.)

Thaddeus A. Ledbetter
STILL UNDEFEATED!!

PRISON JOURNAL, CONTINUED

DAY 10:

- I didn't make entries for a few days, since they took my computer away. Some nonsense about me not using it for the educational reasons intended. Yeah right, the world needs another report on Dolly Madison.

- Stayed busy. I had a dentist appointment, and he told me that one of my baby molars hadn't fallen out and the adult one underneath was trying to come in. He gave me ten days to wiggle it out or he was going to remove it himself. I didn't like the sound of that, and my mom said she wasn't paying a dentist to do it, so I got to wiggling.

- Apparently, Mrs. Calhoun (and also Shirley from her phone conversations) has a bit of a tooth-losing phobia. I'd be all wiggling my tooth—"doctor's orders," I'd tell her—and she'd get all white-faced and excuse herself. It was great!

- When it finally popped out, there was a lot of blood. More than I expected. This just sent Mrs. Calhoun over the edge, screaming, acting like she was going to pass out, and hitting the Emergency button to the office.

- She then told Mr. Cooper to give me my computer back to keep me busy. She wasn't going to stay in ISS if I was just going to sit around every day yanking out teeth. Therefore, I'm back in business.

- Nachos for lunch.

DAY 11:

- Wrote some more blues songs. I think I'm getting really good at it. I read one to Mrs. Calhoun, and she said blues songs can't be about weenie dogs. What does she know? Maybe she would appreciate them more if I sang them, though I really don't have that cool, raspy blues voice yet. I wonder if it would help if I drank some whiskey or smoked a cigar. I asked my mom to get me some whiskey at the grocery store, but she declined.
- Nachos for lunch.

DAY 12:

- Worked on my explanation of the slug-bug incident. I'm thinking I'll need to fully explain how slug-bugging works so Mr. Cooper will understand how the heat of competition can fog the situation, though heat usually clears fog. That's a strange metaphor.
- Sounds like Shirley's digestive problems are back. Mrs. Calhoun seems to think you can fix any malady with more fiber.
- Just realized that I did not include the isolated ISS room in my True Emergency Drill. If disaster struck, where would Mrs. Calhoun and I go for safety? If she is going to freak out from a little blood from a loose tooth, what is she going to do in a real disaster? I had better make myself the Disaster Room Captain.
- Made myself Disaster Room Captain.
- See, this is why I ran the drill in the first place, to find the

weaknesses in our system and correct them. I'm going to start working on a plan in case a plane crashes into the school. Maybe a giant trampoline on the roof? Though it would be difficult to keep the kids off of it. And pilots might find it tempting to hit the trampoline just for fun. I need to give this some more thought.

DAY 13:

- Finally heard back from Uncle Pete. Sounds like Mr. Dunham, a.k.a. "The Slug Bug," is still all worked up. I need to get my defense done so that everyone will see it was a misunderstanding and that I am not at fault. He might as well sue the sky for raining.

- I hope I'm not grounded this weekend. It sounds like Alison's mom really needs my help with something. She has this weird way of hinting that she needs something by acting like she wants to help ME with something. Yeah, right, like I need her help. So hopefully I can spend some time over there fixing what she needs this weekend.

- Nachos for lunch (need to get more lunch money from Mom).

DAY 14:

- Explained the chain of events that caused Mr. Dunham to hit himself with a bus. The more I think about this, the more obvious it is I'm not at fault.

- Apparently the fiber worked for Shirley.

- Forgot to get lunch money. No nachos. Had to eat a PB&J sandwich. Yuck. I remember in the fourth grade learning about George Washington Carver and all his peanut discoveries. I wonder if he intended for his life's work to be used to torture kids who forgot their lunch money.

DAY 15:

- Billy wanted me to write a paper for him for five bucks. I really could use the money (no more PB&J sandwiches!!!), and how hard can it be? You could shave a monkey, give it a typewriter, and it could write a paper people would believe was written by Billy. Actually, you wouldn't even have to shave it. Billy's really hairy for a seventh-grader. Shoot, he's really hairy for a human.

DAY 16:

- Time went by REALLY slow today. Boy, I hope Uncle Pete comes to dinner this weekend. He's so busy, it's hard to get a hold of him. He said he might take me to the museum, but I'm not sure I want to go there yet. This is where I went with my dad. Maybe I'll go to Alison's house so her mother will stop bothering me.

Thaddeus,

I have read your explanation of the incident with Mr. Dunham (I really didn't need another copy of your résumé). In no way does your explanation excuse what you did, or mitigate the seriousness of the event. But I did get the impression that you truly believe you did nothing wrong. To be honest, I don't know how to respond to this.

Young man, I will give you some advice that you really need to take. When asking people to help you, I would refrain from insulting them, calling their competency into question, and using an overall tone of condescension. Even if you are making valid points, they are lost in your presentation.

And Thaddeus, please do not make it difficult for Mrs. Calhoun. I would appreciate if you kept your teeth to yourself. She needs to make it through this year and then she can retire.

Mr. Cooper

Dear Mr. Armstrong,

Or if you prefer, Stinkear. What is the proper way of addressing blues singers? Surname or nickname? And does the nickname always have to be based on a physical deformity? What if the artist is sensitive about it? I don't think anyone would want to be known as "Pimply Face," "Gouty," or "Lingering, Undefinable Body Odor." Is there some sort of rule book or governing body for blues names?

Anyway, I'm writing because Mr. Kessel, this accountant I knew but who is now in prison (which would make a pretty good blues song, now that I think about it), was always listening to your music.

At first, I thought it all sounded the same and boring. But because of recent events in my life, I can feel the blues like you wouldn't believe. I've even written a couple of blues songs that I'd like you to look at. I don't know how to write music, but it sounds like you play the same music for every song, so I figure it doesn't matter. They're called:

> "I'm So Bored That My Ears Fell Off Blues"
> "My Weenie Dog Is Chasing the Devil"
> "I Asked for Nachos and They Gave Me PB&J"

Maybe we could do an album together. Should I send them to this address?

Thaddeus "Babytooth" Ledbetter

THE UNKNOWN DANGERS
OF NUTRITION

Discipline Referral Form

Student's Name: Thaddeus Ledbetter   Grade: 7   Gender: M

Teacher's Name: _____

Location of Offense: off-site _____

Reason(s) for Referral

He lured my Scout troop into truancy and TRIED TO KILL OLD PEOPLE!!!

Previous Corrective Action(s) Taken by Teacher

☐ Student Conference _____ Times   ☐ Referred to Counselor

☒ Time-Out/Loss of Privilege   ☐ Behavior Contract

☒ Seating Change   ☐ Letter Sent Home

☐ Phone Conference with Parent

☐ Face-to-Face Conference with Parent

☐ Other _____

Action(s) Taken by Administrator

☐ Discussion   ☐ Verbal Reprimand

☒ Warning/Probation   ☐ Referred to Counselor

☐ Student Conference   ☐ Detention

☐ Contacted Parent   ☐ In-School Suspension (ISS)

☐ Detention   ☐ Expulsion

☐ D.A.E.P. Assignment   ☐ Referral to Law Enforcement

☐ Other _____

Administrator Signature Principal Frank Cooper _____

Student Signature Thaddeus A. Ledbetter (soon to be Esq.) _____

DEFENSE

PERCEIVED DISCIPLINARY ACCUSATION #2:

Encouraging truancy and endangering senior citizens.

ACTUAL EVENT:

Encouraging good nutrition for both the student body
and the older generation.

. . . .

First of all, Mr. Cooper, this did not happen on school grounds,
so why are you involved? I realize this happened during the
school day, but is it your responsibility? Isn't Scout Leader Hardy
just passing the buck to you? Are you going to let him push you
around like that?

Anyway, since both of you insist on being involved, let me
explain. Truth be told, this accusation is a crime against justice
even worse than the slug-bug incident.

Speaking of the real world, I've got another great idea for
how to make the school run better. As you know, you made the
decision that I'm not allowed on campus anymore, so I'm unable
to put suggestions in your suggestion box. Therefore, I will use
some of my valuable defense space to give them to you now
(further evidence of how much I value this school, and how value
should be reciprocated).

THADDEUS A. LEDBETTER
DEFENSE

> ### A Thaddeus Fun Fact
> The word "reciprocate" comes from the Latin *reciprocus*, meaning "returning the same way." In other words, it's the old "you scratch my back, I'll scratch yours." Except there probably won't be any literal scratching between us. I'm pretty sure the school board would frown on that much physical contact.

I got this idea while working on my defense of the so-called slug-bug incident. You remember how the bus driver, Mr. Hines, freaked out and made that man hit himself with the bus? Now that I think about it, one could argue that it was these two guys who did all the damage. So why am I making the defense?

But since I am, here's an excellent idea that could keep poor drivers and irrational large people from causing damage to themselves and the public. The best way to survive a disaster is a good disaster prevention plan. What if Mr. Hines hadn't freaked out? What if he had just waited for the light to change and then driven away in a normal fashion? Then we would have just had an irrationally mad, large man safely outside the area of the bus and not hurting himself. So as to prevent another episode of fat man vs. bus, I redesigned the basic school bus layout so that the driver can have an assistant—a "wingman" I believe they are referred to in military parlance.

For this illustration, we'll call the wingman "Thaddeus," just for the ease of clarity. (I would be willing to consider the position.)

Interior of New, "Safety First" Bus

With the added help and lessened distractions, the bus driver will be free to concentrate on not hitting angry fat guys with his mirror.

Riders are arranged by smartest to dumbest to limit distractions to driver

(last seat reserved for Billy Cunningham)

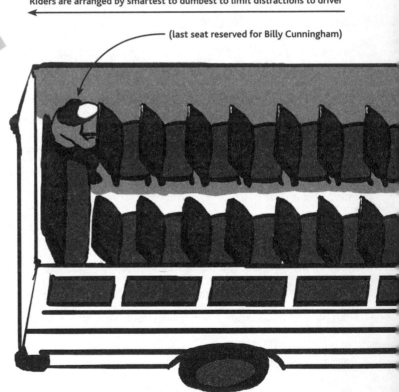

WINGMAN'S WORK SPACE INCLUDES:

- direct line walkie-talkie to driver for directions, speed recommendations, interesting historical markers and Fun Facts, as well as general tips as wingman thinks necessary

- buzzer to indicate to driver when to stop (possibly an extra brake pedal like they have in driver's ed cars for rookie drivers who need a lot of help)

- megaphone for communicating to dullards in back of bus (maybe Taser for unruly passengers)

- clipboard to organize assigned seating

- label maker to label seats to official rider

- police radio to call in infractions (i.e., not sitting in assigned seat, attacks by irrational fat people, driver not spending the prescribed amount of time stopped before crossing railroad tracks, etc.)

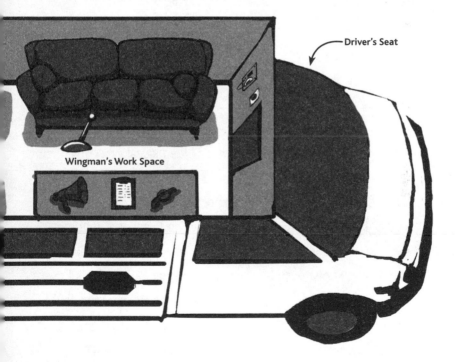

Driver's Seat

Wingman's Work Space

Crooked Creek Middle School
STUDENT INFORMATION FILE

Student File Cont.

<u>1/30</u> In one of the strangest, most ironic, and slightly disturbing submissions of my career as a principal, Thaddeus has spent time in ISS rewriting the discipline referral form. This is like a mouse taking the initiative to make a better mousetrap. Of course, it has his unique slant on things and is completely useless in the classroom (I truly believe the teachers would riot if I tried to implement this during a faculty meeting). Still, once you get past the over-the-top aspects, it does have some interesting ideas in it. (See attached.)

Mr. Cooper,

I have come to the realization that one of the biggest problems with your discipline plan for our school is that the focus is on dumb things like worksheet completion and remembering to bring a pencil to class. Here's an idea: let's actually focus on things that matter. Yeah, I know it's a crazy idea around here and teachers get all mad when you bring it up, but let's give it a shot. Plus, it shows how much I care about our school, another mitigating circumstance that should be added to a very long list that will get me out of ISS.

And I relinquish all rights and privileges to this work (and ONLY this work) and give the school full use of it without the need

of compensation to the Thaddeus Ledbetter Corporation.

Discipline Referral Form

Student name: _____

Grade: _____ Today's date:_____ Date of alleged offense:_____

Name of teacher making "accusation": _____

Location of "offense": _____

Student verifier: _____

Reason for Referral

◯ Misuse of important-student lane

◯ Distracting wingman on bus

◯ Misuse of subject pronouns

◯ Displaying gross stupidity by saying, "How can I look it up if I can't spell it?"

◯ Cheating at Slug Bug

◯ Making someone hit himself

◯ Referring to squiggles as art

◯ Misuse of citrus

◯ Freaking out during emergency drills

◯ Improper disposal of nachos

◯ Other (please explain) _____

_____

_____

Actions Taken by Administrator

◯ Punishment to be determined by Thaddeus A. Ledbetter,
   discipline coordinator

◯ No nachos for a week

◯ 50 worksheets that teach nothing

◯ Water ballooning by student body

◯ Bite from Brown Recluse spider

◯ Weenie dog mauling (extreme cases only)

But back to my defense. You remember how we always have a week where we are supposed to raise the awareness of and revel in the celebration of good nutrition? Well, I've got to tell you, you all did a horrible job this year. Who's in charge of planning this event anyway?

In previous years, we had an exotic-fruit-tasting party, a "you are what you eat" essay contest (my essay detailing how I must have some Mexican blood in me because of my love of nachos, the "king of foods," was immediately and illegally disqualified, and I have yet to hear a plausible explanation of why), and were served tofu "turkey." OK, the turkey wasn't that great of an idea, but we kids appreciated the effort (except that one who was allergic and got violently ill in the hall. But how could you have known? So I'll let you slide on that one).

Well, guess what we got this year to celebrate nutrition? You know how our cafeteria fruit cups are generally made up of little pieces of pears, peaches, pineapples, and white grapes? (Wait . . . I've never seen you eat any of the food you serve the student body in the cafeteria. You're not hoarding a secret stash of the good food in your office, are you? If it weren't for the nacho line, I'd probably have a backup eating plan, too.)

Anyway, those four fruits are what make up our fruit cups. But to celebrate Nutrition Week this year, they also included little pieces of apricot! Yes, that mysterious, delicious food from the world of Apricotania!

THADDEUS A. LEDBETTER
DEFENSE

No, wait, let me rephrase that: For Nutrition Week, we got a couple of little chunks of apricot added to the syrupy glop referred to as a fruit cup. I can't express how underwhelmed we were.

So I conducted a little man-on-the-street survey during that lunch. See attached:

Actual responses to the query
"How do you feel about the fact that the only way we celebrated Nutrition Week this year was to have apricots in the fruit cups?":

"What are you talking about?"

"Thaddeus, please just leave me alone and let me enjoy my
   sloppy joe."

"What's an apricot?"

"Get away from me, FREAK."

"Do you know if we're having a notebook check today in
   Mrs. Garza's class?"

"You smell like a wet dog."

"If you don't want it, I'll take your fruit cup."

"Yo, Nacho Boy, why do you care anyway?"

"How about a punch in the throat?"

"Can you do a pull-up yet?"

"Are you still talking?"

THADDEUS A. LEDBETTER
DEFENSE

The Apricot: the eager-beaver fruit that can't.

A Thaddeus Fun Fact

The word "apricot" comes from the Catalan word *abercoc*, which means "early ripening." If your only name-worthy quality is being the first to ripen, you don't have a lot going for you. This fruit is pretty much the natural world's equivalent of the kid who always shows up early to class and then does no classwork, fails out of school, and lives under the overpass. (I've noticed we don't have many words from Catalan, which leads me to believe it may be a made-up country, or if it does exist, it is cursed with bad fruit.)

Mr. Cooper, as you have said at many inspirational assemblies, "When life gives you lemons, make lemonade." If only I had a lemon instead of a stupid apricot (see Fun Fact below), I would have been happy. But I decided to correct the apricot mistake of what was so erroneously referred to as "Nutrition Week" by actually helping people with their nutrition.

A Thaddeus Fun Fact

People say "When life gives you lemons, make lemonade." Why? Life's never given me anything at all, except for a dad who gets sick and dies. I'd be happy with a lemon. Shoot, I like lemons. You can use the juice for invisible ink, or put a slice in your water on a hot day.

THADDEUS A. LEDBETTER
DEFENSE

As luck would have it, during Nutrition Week, Scout Leader Hardy told our troop he wanted us to do a service project at the Crooked Creek Nursing Home just three blocks down from the school. This was serendipity.

A Thaddeus Fun Fact

"Serendipity" is a term coined by this guy named Horace Walpole back in the 1700s. There's this ridiculous story about princes and lions, and this weird thing about a lame, one-eyed camel behind it that's really more weird than interesting called "The Three Princes of Serendip." This Walpole guy actually stole the story from an old Italian guy who had stolen it from an old Persian story. They weren't really interested in copyright laws back then. But these princes were always getting lucky in unexpected ways, so instead of having to go through that long story, we just use "serendipity" to describe when something cool happens. In that same vein, I keep expecting "Thaddipity" to catch on for "stroke of genius."

I was in the kitchen asking Mrs. Wilkes, the cafeteria lady, if she had anything to do with this Nutrition Week travesty, when I saw this giant bag of oranges in the corner. I inquired about them and was informed that there had been a mistake in the order and an extra shipment of oranges had been delivered and she didn't know what to do with them.

Apparently, if you add apricots AND oranges to a fruit cup, it is no longer a "fruit cup," but a "fruit medley," and a medley is not on the official school menu. If it's not on the official menu, it can't be served. And since there weren't enough for each student to have an entire orange, she really had no way to serve them.

Then it hit me. "You know who would love these oranges?" I said to myself. "The folks at the Crooked Creek Nursing Home. They'd get a Nutrition Week treat (much better than us kids), and we Scouts could get our service badges. That would be killing two birds with one stone."

Mr. Cooper, let me be clear, I was speaking to myself figuratively here, and no actual birds were killed during this process. I know how you work. I don't want to find out later that you are punishing me for some ridiculous bird massacre.

Please note how antiquated this form is. Please implement mine immediately.

Time was of the essence. I don't know how long it takes oranges to go bad, but since it was a Thursday, and I didn't want them to go bad over the weekend (it's impossible to schedule activities on Fridays with these kids. I have yet to have anyone show up to a single club meeting I've scheduled on a Friday), I needed to act right away.

So I went back in the cafeteria and found James Roe, Taylor Allen, and some other of my fellow Scouts and told them that we had been ordered to take the oranges to the nursing home. We were on DEFCON 1, Alert Level Red. Operation Fruit Exchange was a go.

Of course, they had no idea what those words meant, but I have found if I make it sound important and use military phrases, Scouts follow orders much more quickly.

Crooked Creek Discipline Referral Form

INNOCENT STUDENT UNJUSTLY ACCUSED:
Thaddeus A. Ledbetter

MADE-UP OFFENSE:
Miraculously throwing a single stone with such accuracy and coincidence that two birds were knocked out of the sky and brutally killed.

PUNISHMENT:
Lifelong In-School Suspension, unless the school board incorporates a capital punishment provision.

SIGNATURE: Dictator-for-Life Cooper

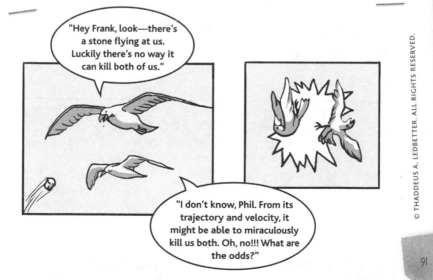

THADDEUS A. LEDBETTER

DEFENSE

A Thaddeus Fun Fact

"DEFCON" stands for "defense readiness condition" and is used by the Department of Defense to indicate the readiness to fight by our armed forces. And to put it in nontechnical vernacular, it uses a scale of 5, where "Wow, looks like the rest of the world is out of bullets. Let's take a nap" would be a 5, and "I think I just saw an enemy soldier punch the president. Maybe we should use these tanks and planes in an extreme manner" would be a 1. We spend most of our time at DEFCON 3: "Hey, that country is giving us the stink-eye, so watch your back."

OK, so maybe here I took a tiny liberty. No one had officially ordered us, in so many words at least, to take the oranges to the nursing home. But I remember once overhearing Mrs. Garza saying to another teacher that in education, sometimes it's more effective to ask for forgiveness rather than ask permission.

Plus, you are always talking about character. Instead of doing another dumb worksheet in class after lunch, we were actually finding a way to use our positive traits: generosity, responsibility, initiative, and resourcefulness.

So my fellow Scouts and I went into the kitchen to get the oranges, exited out the back door, and walked a few blocks to the nursing home.

A Thaddeus Fun Fact

It is a proven fact that pets and children make the blood pressure of octogenarians go down and make the elderly healthier. I suppose it is because they are smaller than old people. Makes you wonder if a dwarf or midget (they prefer to be called "little people") would have the same effect. Maybe that's why circus folk live so long.

THADDEUS A. LEDBETTER
DEFENSE

When we arrived at the nursing home, I explained to the nurse at the front desk why we were there. She started flipping through her schedule and said she could find no record of our appointment, but I explained that due to the excitement of Nutrition Week, there must have been some sort of paperwork snafu.

Now, technically, not having asked for the paperwork is, in a sense, a type of snafu, so this really wasn't a lie, so just calm down.

A Thaddeus Fun Fact

I thought this would be a good place to explain the etymology of "SNAFU," but after looking it up, I don't think it would help my case. Let's just say that guys in the army sometimes use inappropriate language. That really seems out of character for them. Maybe they were having a bad war when they came up with this acronym.

When the secretary was hesitant to let us see the residents, I had my business card with me. Seeing my obviously high rank in the Boy Scouts finally convinced her to let us in.

We were led into a recreation room where residents were watching TV or playing bingo. Basically, they were just sitting there. There was very little energy in the room, and they obviously could have used some better nutrition.

THADDEUS A. LEDBETTER
(soon to be Esq.)

SCHOLAR · LEADER · FUTURE LAWYER
FIRST CLASS BOY SCOUT (SOON TO BE EAGLE SCOUT)

BLUES ARTIST

WEENIE DOG WHISPERER

MEMBER OF
11 GROUPS, CLUBS,
& ORGANIZATIONS

EFFICIENCY EXPERT

DISASTER-PREVENTION
SPECIALIST

Hey Thadman,

Sorry you couldn't make it to my movie party last weekend. It was the bomb! We watched this scary movie and Julie Houseman started screaming and hiding her head in the pillows. It was hilarious.

I missed how you like to point out how impossible it would be to have a monster walking around eating people without the proper authorities being called, or when you say things like if people acted as stupidly as the ones in the movie do, they deserve to be eaten. The other kids didn't seem to miss you as much. Andrew said you're a "mood killer" when watching movies, but I told him he didn't know what he was talking about.

As usual, my mom insisted I say she says "hello" and hopes you get out of ISS soon. Got to get back to my history essay. (Billy wants to know if you're done with his yet.)

Peace, Alison

THADDEUS A. LEDBETTER

Dear Mr. Kessel,

I hope this letter finds you well. I didn't know your prison number, so I didn't include it in the address. Is it on the front of your prison suit like in the old movies? Speaking of prison, how are things? What day is nacho day in the Big House? By the way, this is Thaddeus, the kid who lived on the floor above you who used to listen to the blues with you before you went to prison for stealing that dry cleaner's money.

Guess what, I'm in prison, too. It's a long, horrible story of injustice. Though, I truly am innocent—you know, in the REALLY innocent way, not the way you said you were "innocent" when trying not to get convicted. Having the dry cleaner's money in your account in the Bahamas didn't help your case.

Anyway, I wanted to let you know that I'm still into the blues, probably even more now that I'm in the Big House. How about you?

I've even been writing some blues songs myself. I sent some to your favorite singer, Stinkear Armstrong. There are songs about my weenie dog, and your ears falling off because you're bored. You know, the usual blues topics. I haven't heard back from him yet, but that makes sense. Always being broke, lonely, and having "The Man" keeping him down probably makes him slow at correspondence.

THADDEUS A. LEDBETTER

I've written another song that I thought you might appreciate (see attached). I've also been trying to learn the harmonica, as I'm sure you are, too, since that's what you do in prison.

Doing hard time,
Thaddeus "Babytooth" Ledbetter (future Esq.)
CCMS-ISS (Solitary confinement division)
P.S. I also enclosed a safety poster from my Citrus Kills campaign

The Man Is Keeping Me Down with His Citrus

(A Blues Song by Thaddeus "Babytooth" Ledbetter)

I should have known better
But it looked so sweet
I had a sandwich, but wanted something wetter
And it was the Man's citrus that kicked me in the seat

That ol' orange is gonna kill ya, baby
Maybe even that tangerine
Especially if you ain't got no choppers
It's the most dangerous fruit ever seen

(yow-yow-yow-yow, with occasional "oh yeah")

Then I saw my granny there
Really needing to be refreshed
I should have gone with a pear
But it was citrus that was best

That ol' orange is gonna kill ya, baby
Maybe even that tangerine
Especially if you ain't got no choppers
It's the most dangerous fruit ever seen

(slurping and choking noises in rhythm)

THADDEUS A. LEDBETTER
DEFENSE

We started handing out oranges, and though the residents seemed happy to get them (it was really hard to tell), we noticed that no one was eating. Then I realized that they might have trouble peeling them, so I instructed my fellow Scouts to start helping them peel. Otherwise, we might as well have given them rubber balls to play with.

Then I realized that to get the Boy Scout service badge, we'd need proof for Scout Leader Hardy, so I went looking for someone with a camera. I figured it would also be a good photo-op for the paper for one of those "See, not all kids are writing graffiti and/or playing video games all day" stories.

After asking around, I finally found a nurse who had a camera in her car and went to get it. When I got back to the rec room, many of the residents had the peeled oranges in their laps, but no one was eating them. What kind of caption would there be for that picture? "The residents of Crooked Creek Nursing Home enjoy holding their peeled oranges for no apparent reason."

So I told my Scouts to help these people eat their oranges. If we timed it right, they'd be right in the middle of a delicious slice when the nurse got there with her camera. The enjoyment would be reflected in their faces, and the vitamin C coursing through their bodies would fill them with energy. The ultimate photo opportunity. What a wonderful plan!

THADDEUS A. LEDBETTER
DEFENSE

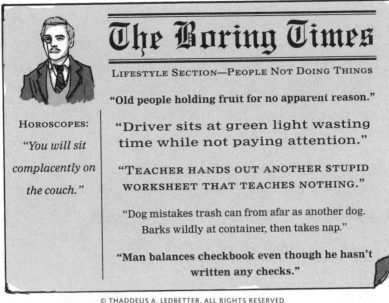

The Boring Times

LIFESTYLE SECTION—PEOPLE NOT DOING THINGS

"Old people holding fruit for no apparent reason."

HOROSCOPES:

"You will sit complacently on the couch."

"Driver sits at green light wasting time while not paying attention."

"TEACHER HANDS OUT ANOTHER STUPID WORKSHEET THAT TEACHES NOTHING."

"Dog mistakes trash can from afar as another dog. Barks wildly at container, then takes nap."

"Man balances checkbook even though he hasn't written any checks."

OK, maybe there was one flaw that I could not have possibly foreseen. We were all gently feeding tiny, bite-size morsels into the residents' mouths when the nurse walked in and started freaking out and screaming. It turns out she is another one of those adults who immediately escalates to screaming at the drop of a hat. Kind of like you, Mr. Cooper . . . and the bus driver and Mrs. Calhoun, now that I think about it.

Once that lady started yelling, everything fell apart. Turns out (and again, there is no way for anyone to have known this) people of a certain age don't have teeth except at their scheduled eating times. Yes, you read that correctly: People don't have their teeth in their head at all times.

When you think about it, that's really interesting. I'm wondering what other body parts are optional and/or removable at your leisure. I think I'd like to be able to take off my ears when all the yelling starts (if they haven't already detached from being so bored), which seems to be on a daily basis around here. Or maybe detachable eyebrows? Maybe there are some situations in which you don't want to register surprise, anger, or other emotions? The more I think about it, that would be cool, and possibly quite advantageous.

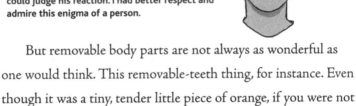

Is he mad? Maybe bewildered? Pensive? Could it possibly be gas? I just can't tell. Hmmmm, he's quite mysterious. If only he had eyebrows so I could judge his reaction. I had better respect and admire this enigma of a person.

But removable body parts are not always as wonderful as one would think. This removable-teeth thing, for instance. Even though it was a tiny, tender little piece of orange, if you were not in possession of your teeth, it's a bit tricky.

So that's where we were at: five Scouts trying to help their elders with nutrition, and a shrieking nurse upsetting the residents. That's when the mass choking began.

The funny thing about choking (obviously funny-weird, not funny-ha-ha) is that people who are choking don't make any noise. If you add the fact that if the person choking doesn't know the international sign for choking, the hand to the throat, well then it was an even bigger problem.

DEFENSE

However, as Scouts, we are highly trained experts in emergency first-aid. "Gentlemen," I said, "this is not a drill. Assume the Heimlich position." Since we were in front of the patients pumping in orange slices, it would be a quick maneuver to slide behind them and give them first aid.

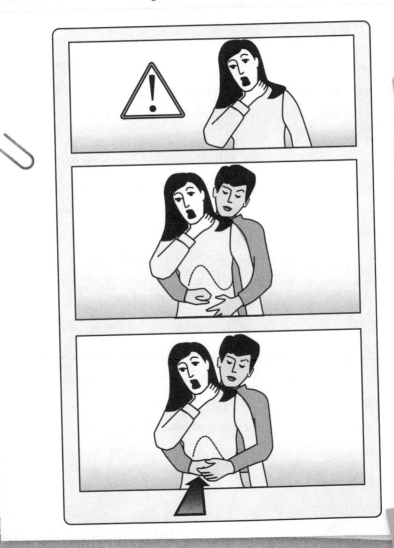

But as we were responding to the emergency at hand (I was, at least; the other guys were just kind of standing there stunned), the nurse starts shouting, "Don't touch them! Get away from them! You've done enough damage!!"

"Whoa, calm down, lady! Remember, we're Scouts. We've got this under control."

I explain to her, but she is so busy shouting "Code Red! Code Red!" into the intercom that she doesn't hear me. Suddenly, all these orderlies burst in, one pushes me away, and they very crudely perform the exact same Heimlich maneuver we were about to do perfectly.

Wow! I don't believe I have ever seen adults who so needed to be the center of attention! We had the situation all under control, yet they had to take over so they could be the heroes. Kind of pathetic, actually.

After everyone finally calmed down, I gave the orderlies a few technique tips for rescuing chokers (they weren't very receptive, which explains why they do it so poorly) and even tried to show the residents how to perform the Heimlich on themselves in case they are ever caught in a citrus/no-teeth situation again.

It was about this time when Scout Leader Hardy showed up and the shouting started all over again. And geesh, when I asked the nurse when we were going to take the picture, you would have thought I asked when I could light the whole place on fire. Maybe you and she could start an Overreactors of America club.

THADDEUS A. LEDBETTER
DEFENSE

FYI, Mr. Cooper (since you are getting up there in years), if you find yourself in a similar situation, there are two ways to save yourself from choking:

A) Make a fist and punch yourself in the stomach. Even if you don't dislodge food, people will notice you pummeling yourself and note that you are in trouble (unless it's Billy, and he'll ask, "Why are you punching yourself?" and use your other arm to punch your shoulder).

B) Lean against a chair violently and repeatedly. After saving yourself, you can also take this opportunity to rearrange the furniture.

You know what happens next. But now that you know the facts and motivations, I'm sure you feel remorseful. It's OK, I forgive you.

The life you save may be your grandmother's!

WARNING:
The Elderly and Citrus Do Not Mix!!
Citrus Kills!

So keep it away from your older loved ones.

Brought to you by the Citrus Safety Counsel · President Thaddeus A. Ledbetter

CITRUS LEAGUE *of* **AMERICA**

Mr. Herb Ratliff

President

Citrus League of America

1019 Citrus Way, Suite E

Sunnyside, FL 50090

November 2

Mr. Thaddeus Ledbetter,

We are contacting you regarding your "Citrus Kills" campaign. The citrus growers of America are not endangering the elderly as your flyers, posters, and Web site suggest. We don't feel your representation of our product is at all accurate. It is not just wrong, it is offensive. If you do not cease and desist in your inflammatory campaign immediately, we will pursue legal action.

Sincerely,

Herb Ratliff

THADDEUS A. LEDBETTER

Thaddeus A. Ledbetter (future Esq.)
Crooked Creek Middle School

November 4

Mr. Herb Ratliff,

Get bent. I'm saving lives here! Any further correspondence should be directed to my lawyer, Peter Ledbetter.

Sincerely,
Thaddeus A. Ledbetter

Sent: November 5

From: Peter.Ledbetter@awlassociates.com

To: thaddeus.ledbetter@ccms.edu

Thaddeus,

The Citrus League's lawyers have given you 48 hours to cease and desist. I want you to go take down all of your "Citrus Kills" posters and flyers immediately!!!!

Also, Pastor Snodgrass has left me 8 messages. I'm afraid to call back. Please stop getting in trouble. PLEASE.

Uncle Pete

Crooked Creek
CHURCH

September 3

Mr. Cooper,

I'm writing to let you know that my mentoring organization, Shaping Tomorrow's Minds, will again be sending volunteers to your campus. I believe we helped a lot of kids last year.

We'll have our first meeting next week to introduce ourselves to the kids. Remembering what happened last year, will you please remind Thaddeus Ledbetter that he can be involved, but as a mentee, not a mentor?

I will try to involve Thaddeus in my church. We're always looking to bring the wayward back to the flock, and though Thaddeus may not be wayward, he definitely wants to go his own way.

Best Regards,
Pastor Lawrence Snodgrass

Hey Thad-a-lad,

You remember the first thing you said to me back in sixth grade when we met? Something like, "After three applications just in this class, your lips should be incredibly moisturized. You should also know lip balm is the perfect breeding ground for germs."

I remember thinking that you were the weirdest kid I have ever met, and I was right. Still, I can't believe I won't see you the rest of the year.

Class is so boring without you. OK, sometimes you're a little annoying, and *weird*, but what boy isn't? Will you be ungrounded this weekend? I'm thinking about going skating. Tell your mom hi for me.

Enjoy your nachos.

TTFN,
Alison

PRISON JOURNAL, CONTINUED

DAY 17:

- Uncle Pete brought dinner Friday night. Fried chicken!! A nice chicken leg is the only food that can even compare to nachos. He lives about an hour away, is real busy with his legal career, and has kids of his own. His daughters, my cousins, are kind of weird and never want to do anything cool when we get together. They have this deck behind their house that must have a million spiders underneath it, but heaven forbid we crawl around underneath to find some. They start shrieking if I just bring it up.

- He does have a son who seems pretty cool. He's only two right now, but he enjoys going in the backyard and finding bugs. Plus, he takes direction well. There's hope for him yet.

- Anyway, it was great to see him and nice to have a fellow man in the house for a few hours to discuss manly things. He hasn't made the progress on my case I had hoped, but I gave him copies of my defense and other pertinent paperwork.

- One strange thing happened. I was in the bathroom washing my hands, and I thought I overheard Mom and Uncle Pete talking about my dad. When I walked out, my mom was crying. She pretended she wasn't, but I could tell she was. I know she doesn't like me to see her cry, so I pretended not to notice. I know she misses Dad as much as I do. Sometimes, I wish we could talk about it.

- Uncle Pete told me to be strong and the man of the house, and I told him I would. But I get tired of being strong sometimes.

DAY 18:

- Spent most of the day reading this great science magazine Uncle Pete brought me. It has this cool article about how only about 40,000 of the more than 100,000 spiders on the planet have been identified and named. I should be able to find an undiscovered one in the building basement very easily.
- Leftover fried chicken for lunch again. Delicious.

DAY 19:

- Got a letter from the Citrus League of America and was surprised when it wasn't an offer of leadership, or at least, membership. Apparently my "Citrus Kills" campaign got their attention. Hey, if they want to be merchants of death, I guess they have the right. But I also have the right to try to stop them. I did write back, and to be blunt, I was blunt.
- My dad always said it's important to fight the good fight, even if you know you are going to lose, so I'm fighting it.
- Nachos for lunch (it's good to be back).

DAY 20:

- Need to talk to Uncle Pete, but have to be careful. The whole citrus defense made him mad. Really mad. I didn't know you could scream through an e-mail.
- I may need to do some schoolwork in the next couple of days.

- Mrs. Wilkes brought another note from Alison. You know, for a girl, she's really kind of cool. I'm so bored, I'd even enjoy going to her house and helping with one of their dumb problems that need fixing.
- Nachos for lunch.

DAY 21:
- Almost got my defense of the citrus incident done. I don't think people know how this silent killer (literally, since you don't make a noise while choking) is affecting our elderly population.
- Will do schoolwork tomorrow, really! Maybe if I bring home some good grades, Mom will unground me.

DAY 22:
- Finished Citrus Defense and will send it to Mr. Cooper. May also "CC" copies to Uncle Pete and Citrus League. It's time they stopped deluding themselves.
- Got ten math problems done. Found greatest common denominator. At least we're focusing on the most important numbers now.
- Mrs. Calhoun says Shirley is under the weather. What a strange expression. Aren't we all under the weather all the time? Except for maybe astronauts, who are above the weather. This may be a good Fun Fact. I told her to tell Shirley to eat more fiber. She agreed this was good advice.
- Nachos are especially good today.

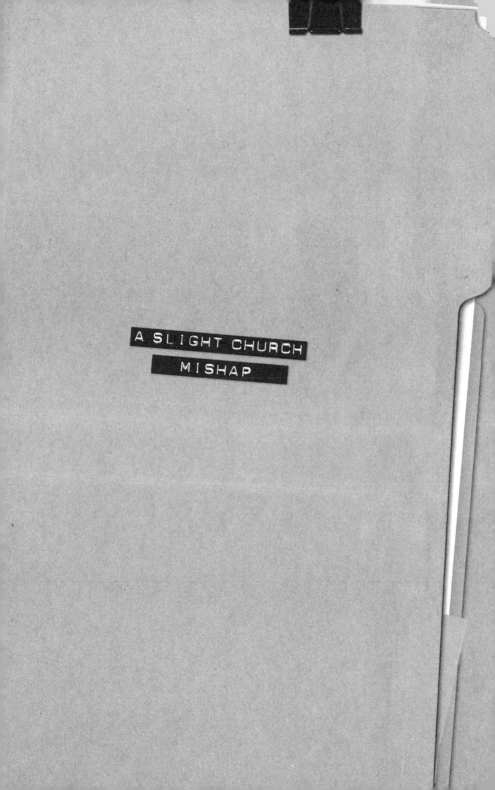

A SLIGHT CHURCH
MISHAP

Discipline Referral Form

Student's Name: _Thaddeus Ledbetter_____ Grade: _7_ Gender: _M_

Teacher's Name: _____

Location of Offense: _off-site_____

Reason(s) for Referral

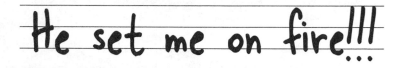

He set me on fire!!!...

Previous Corrective Action(s) Taken by Teacher

☐ Student Conference _____ Times   ☐ Referred to Counselor

☒ Time-Out/Loss of Privilege   ☐ Behavior Contract

☒ Seating Change   ☐ Letter Sent Home

☒ Phone Conference with Parent

☐ Face-to-Face Conference with Parent

☐ Other _____

Action(s) Taken by Administrator

☐ Discussion   ☐ Verbal Reprimand

☒ Warning/Probation   ☐ Referred to Counselor

☐ Student Conference   ☐ Detention

☐ Contacted Parent   ☐ In-School Suspension (ISS)

☐ Detention   ☐ Expulsion

☐ D.A.E.P. Assignment   ☐ Referral to Law Enforcement

☐ Other _____

Administrator Signature _Principal Frank Cooper_____

Student Signature _Thaddeus A. Ledbetter (soon to be Esq.)_____

Thaddeus!

You'll never guess what happened today! Mrs. Garza decided we were going to say the Pledge of Allegiance the way you always did it. Isn't that incredible?!

She used to get so mad at you when you would volunteer to lead the pledge (your "improved" version especially), which was pretty much every day. OK, it was EVERY day, but who's counting among friends? LOL!

She even had a copy of your "A New, Improved, and Vastly More Patriotic Pledge of Allegiance, Copyright Thaddeus A. Ledbetter." How did she get that? And do we have to say all that copyright stuff every time?

Anyway, it was SOOOOOO LIVE! ("Live" is the new word for cool, by the way.) Even though no one admits it, people are starting to miss you.

Alison

Alison,

I'm relieved Mrs. Garza finally came to her senses. I have actually updated the pledge so that it's even more accurate for future pledging.

    Please deliver it to Mrs. Garza.

Regards,

Thaddeus A. Ledbetter, Esq.

A New, Improved, and Vastly More Patriotic

Pledge of Allegiance

(*right hand over heart*) I pledge allegiance (*left hand points to U.S. flag*) to the flag of the United States of America (*wave both arms in circles indicating "all"*), including the District of Columbia, Puerto Rico, and various other islands, which aren't actually states, but should be included. And to the Republic (*raise hand as if voting*), which in this case refers to a form of government, not a particular political party, mind you, so save your letters to the editor, for which it stands (*pointing thumb over shoulder*), and I'm referring back to the above-mentioned "Republic," one nation—that being the United States—under the god of your particular choice, though the one who spoke to Abraham is the most popular in the Western world, indivisible (*make a cutting gesture with hand while shaking head in a "no" fashion*) with liberty and justice for all, except Thaddeus Ledbetter* (*make eye-rubbing, pretend-to-cry motions*).

*Please note new ending

What's happening, Hot Stuff? (Saw a movie with that line in it, so don't get any funny ideas. It was HILARIOUS! When are you going to be able to watch movies again?)

Everybody was excited to get your new pledge in Mrs. Garza's class. Then Teddy Manson asked me to ask you about that thing you always said to Mrs. Sanders in English class that made her so mad. Something about "your" and "their" or something. He says she needs to be put back in her place, and since you're not here to do it, he will. Though I think he's just a lot of big talk. No one has the guts you do when talking to teachers.

Oh yeah, Henry Applecott also wants me to ask you how to make the pencil sharpener do that reverse-spin thing that makes it do those cool grooves in the lead.

Mrs. Sanders keeps threatening us with the "Thaddeus treatment" whenever she gets mad, and says you got what you deserved.

Mrs. Sanders is a loser.

alison

Hey Alison,

Let's do it this way. The next time Mrs. Sanders says "Everyone should take out their books," have Teddy say (and write this down for him exactly, I'm afraid if he goes off script, he'll start yammering about peanut butter crackers or something) "Mrs. Sanders, it should be 'Everyone take out HIS or HER books.' Indefinite pronouns like 'everyone' need singular pronouns. As a supposed English teacher, shouldn't you know this?" At least that's how I would say it.

By the way, is Mrs. Sanders still doing PowerPoint shows for every little lesson so she just has to stand there every period and push a button a few times?

I tried to tell her that PowerPoint stopped being a useful teaching aid when we were in first grade and were still impressed by the cash-register noises and applause sounds, but she keeps using it.

And Alison, Mrs. Sanders isn't a loser. She's just ignorant. And we are obligated to help her.

Thaddeus

P.S. Tell Henry that I will take the pencil-sharpener trick to the grave.

DEFENSE

. . . .

PERCEIVED DISCIPLINARY ACCUSATION #3:
Reckless endangerment of a place of worship

and the worshipers within.

ACTUAL EVENT:
An admirable attempt to increase church attendance.

. . . .

I haven't heard from you after my very reasonable explanation of the slug-bug incident or the citrus incident, so I thought I would address another unfounded accusation. I would have thought you would have picked up on the trend of false accusations directed toward me, but if you need more evidence, so be it.

As you probably noticed on my résumé, I am an ordained acolyte of the Crooked Creek Church. Pastor Snodgrass fast-tracked me to become an acolyte, claiming he had been asked to do so by the school, but I think he saw how valuable I could be to the church.

There are a lot of big words in that last sentence, so I had better explain. First of all, "ordained" means that a governing body recognizes one as being qualified and sanctioned to perform the prescribed duties of the role.

(Whoa, there are even a lot of big words in that explanation. Are you still following me, Mr. Cooper? I'm pretty sure a college-educated man like you can figure it out. Though, was your degree in education? I have to admit, sometimes I'm stunned how little my teachers know. And when you try to inform and/or educate them, they get all huffy.

DEFENSE

And what does one study when getting an education degree? I mean, it's not like math or history, where there are facts to learn. Maybe teachers learn how to write on the board in straight lines or keep an organized notebook.)

Notebook for Mrs. Garza's History Class

Just curious.

She Used to Love Me,
Until I Turned in My Notebook
(A Blues Song by Thaddeus "Babytooth" Ledbetter)

We started so well and she was happy
I could tell 'cause she was always smiling
I was getting worried she might get sappy
But then she started frowning at my filing

Now she don't love me
Don't love me no more
(Sing real fast) 'Course I'm talking about love in the platonic
    sense, not the creepy kind
But it really don't matter
'Cause she hates my notebook at its organizational core

You know I had lots of papers and homework
Not all of them were A's, but I done my best
But I upset her because of some quirk
I happened to put my homework after my test

Oh, mercy
Now she don't love me
Don't love me no more
(Sing real fast) 'Course I'm talking about love in the platonic
    sense, not the creepy kind
But it really don't matter
'Cause she hates my notebook at its organizational core

THADDEUS A. LEDBETTER
DEFENSE

As I was saying, I am an "ordained" acolyte, though, technically, churches don't ordain acolytes, but it's pretty much understood that if they did, I would probably be the first one. So it's more of a de facto ordination. Oh man, I used a Latin phrase. Look, I really don't have time to explain every single word to you, Mr. Cooper, so you can look it up. I also recommend getting one of those "word of the day" calendars. That's how I learned a lot of words myself. (Please see accompanying Fun Fact.)

A Thaddeus Fun Fact

I learned this really cool word from my calendar: "defenestrate." It comes from the Latin *de*, meaning "out of," and *fenestra*, meaning "window," so you get "to throw out of a window." I'm not sure when you would use this word. Maybe if someone discovered a bomb in the room, but if you start shouting, "Defenestrate it!! Defenestrate it!!" he might not know the word and then you would be in trouble. "What are you shouting about? I don't know that word" . . . *KABOOM!!*

But I will explain "acolyte" since it is not used much, especially by the unchurched. Do you go to church? I forgot to ask. If you don't, you should come to ours.

"Acolyte" comes from the Greek *akolouthos*, meaning "following." Don't get the wrong idea about "following." While I am following the pastor in the service, I actually walk in front of him when we enter the sanctuary.

See, I lead the pastor into the sanctuary as the service begins and light the candles with this cool stick thing that I'm trying to find the name for. At the end of the service, I relight my torch, put out the candles, and lead the pastor out of the sanctuary. Basically, the service can't start or end without me.

It's a REALLY important job.

I take my responsibilities of church leadership very seriously, and as you know, I am someone with uncommonly good observation skills, so after a few Sundays, I noticed a lot of empty seats during the services. This is the type of problem I'm great at solving, so I got to thinking about ways to get more people to church, and I approached Pastor Snodgrass with my list.

At first, Pastor Snodgrass was quite open to my suggestions, and he even encouraged my interest in the attendance of our church. I don't know why, but he began to slowly chill to my suggestions, even the ones I'm sure would work.

Like my idea that he should cut down on being so preachy to people. Everyone knows folks don't like being preached at. I mean, it's totally obvious.

Hey Buttface

Where's my paper? If I don't have it by tomorrow morning, it's beating time.

Hey, you didn't narc on me about that fire-drill thing, did you? I will beat you so hard if you try to bring me down with you!!

Some of those nerd kids got all excited about doing your dumb pledge and now are trying to get a petition to get you out of ISS. I'm not signing it.

You know, I kind of miss our weekly beatings. By the way, I killed on Slug Bug when we went to the science museum. Your so-called winning streak is over!

Punch you later, loser,
Billy "Mixed Martial Arts Champ" Cunningham

Hey Thad-Man,

You'll never guess who started a petition to get you out of ISS. James Roeb! Can you believe it? A few of the kids think you were treated unfairly, but mostly, we've noticed we get in a lot more trouble without you here to distract the teacher.

James has already gotten a lot of kids to sign it. Of course, Billy refused because he "don't sign nothing." It's probably better without Billy's signature anyway.

The science museum was sooooo cool. There was this giant tarantula that we got to touch. It was so gross and hairy! You would have loved it.

Hopefully you'll be out soon. I need some help on my science project and school is so much more boring without you. I have to ask how you are doing, you know, for my mom.

Peace out,
Alison

DEFENSE

I had a ton of great ideas. Rather than preaching his sermon every week, what if the preacher discussed his sermon? You know, maybe a little give-and-take. Maybe a roundtable discussion, though we would have to move a pretty big table into the sanctuary. If that proved impractical, how about at least a question-and-answer session. Now that I think about it, it was after this suggestion that Pastor Snodgrass couldn't work me into his schedule anymore.

But I figured it was Pastor Snodgrass's many other demands that kept him from meeting with me. So it became even more important to solve our service attendance problems myself.

A Thaddeus Fun Fact

Guaranteed ways to increase attendance at any church:

1) More guitar solos during hymns, or even better, drum solos.
2) Online poll to update 7 Deadly Sins and 7 Virtues; also create 7 Annoying Pet Peeves and 7 Things That Are Kind of Cool in Small Doses lists for those people who are more comfortable with less judgmental lists.
3) Have a brainteaser in the bulletin for people to think about during the sermon. Maybe also a word search or a Bible story Mad Lib.
4) Bigger portions during Communion.
5) "Bring your pet to church" Sundays (dog people will go just about anywhere if they can bring their dogs).

What I finally decided on was to go for the spectacle. People like big and flashy and sparkly. Think about what big crowds like. When you watch sports events on TV, how do they start the proceedings? With smoke machines, big fireworks spectaculars, and loud rock music as very large men slam into one another repeatedly.

THADDEUS A. LEDBETTER
DEFENSE

Why couldn't we apply this to the worship service, minus the large men slamming? It seemed like the natural fit. Once word got out about the excitement of the service, people would be lining up around the corner to get in, and isn't that the whole point? Folks can't be saved from their bad habits if they're at home watching TV and eating French toast.

My plan was to slowly build up the excitement Sunday to Sunday, to make folks want to be at church to see what was going to happen next. I could just imagine how pleased Pastor Snodgrass would be when the pews started overflowing.

So I decided to get people's attention the first Sunday with something small, just to get them talking, and then add to it each Sunday, building to a full-blown extravaganza.

The Spider Nomenclature Registry

The Smithsonian Institute

Washington, DC, USA

UNDELIVERABLE: ADDRESS NOT FOUND: THE SPIDER NOMENCLATURE REGISTRY

An Exciting Discovery of a New Spider Species

Gentlemen (and ladies, though girls don't seem to like spiders much),

I am happy to report the exciting discovery and naming of a new species of spider. With thousands and thousands of them still to be named, I thought I would help out.

This newly discovered spider, though very similar to *Achaearanea tepidariorum*, or common house spider, is a slightly lighter shade of brown, and obviously one of the unnamed species. I would include a picture of this new species, but I'm afraid the janitor at our building smashed it with his thermos when I was showing it to him in our basement.

As the discoverer of this new species, I have named this species of spider *Thaddeusea ledbetterum*. Please document this in the appropriate manner and form.

Sincerely,

Thaddeus A. Ledbetter

P.S. Please feel free to use my letter as the press release. No need to do another write-up when your time could be better served looking for all these unnamed spiders.

BULLETIN

Pastor: Lawrence Snodgrass

Pastoral Assistant: Susan Goody

Music Director: Lewis Marsh

Choir Director: Laura Marsh

Acolyte: Thaddeus Ledbetter

Liturgist: John Goessleak

Susan, can you change this? I'm sure you understand. I know the good Christian forgives and forgets all, but he set me on fire. Thanks, Pastor Snodgrass

Prayer List

- John Sevier *for his hemorrhoid problem*
- Stu Wolverto *and his strange rash*
- Agatha Simmons *and her vapors*
- Troy Owen *for his giant goiter*

BOY SCOUTS OF AMERICA
★ ★ ★ ★ ★ ★ ★ ★ ★ ★ ★ ★ ★ ★

February 22

Dear First Class Scout Ledbetter,

The district council met to discuss your membership in the Boy Scouts of America. Your lack of attendance at this meeting didn't help your position. And while I understand from your numerous messages that your mother was working and you were not able to find another ride to the meeting, this does not excuse your absence. To be honest, I'm not sure your presence would have helped anyway.

    This letter is to officially inform you that your actions have negatively impacted the community's opinion of your troop. Even though your face was obscured on Channel 7's broadcast of the story, it was clear you were wearing your uniform. Henceforth you are no longer a member of the Boy Scouts of America and should not comport yourself as if you were.

    Thaddeus, as your den leader, this pains me, though you did seem to constantly undermine my authority, and your attitude toward my aunt Gladys has been reprehensible. Still, I wish you the best and hope you take this as a valuable learning lesson. I know you have had a very rough year.

Good luck to you,
Scout Leader William Hardy

P.S. Make sure the Citrus League knows you are in no way affiliated with the Boy Scouts of America.

★ ★ ★ ★ ★ ★ ★ ★ ★ ★ ★ ★

Subject: Last Weekend
Sent: February 25
From: Peter.Ledbetter@awlassociates.com
To: thaddeus.ledbetter@ccms.edu

Hey Thaddeus,

Really enjoyed seeing you and your mother last weekend. I hope you liked the chicken. Next time, I'll bring your cousins.

I've been thinking about your case (the very detailed explanations you have sent me have been informative, though I'm not sure you should send them to the principal—he might take them the wrong way). Maybe your sentence was a little harsh. I'm going to call your principal and see if I can meet with him.

Be strong for your mom. Things will get better at home in time.

Uncle Pete
P.S. Have you named any spiders yet?

THADDEUS A. LEDBETTER
DEFENSE

Step one in progressive church excitement plan: use sparklers for the worship candles. Not that big a deal, but people would notice and it would get the ball rolling. For it to work, it had to be a surprise, so during Sunday school, I excused myself to the bathroom, snuck into the sanctuary between choir practices, and inserted sparklers from my leftover Fourth of July fireworks stash that I keep under my bed.

I got back to my Sunday school class just as things were wrapping up and everyone was doing an Exodus word search. My plan, as usual, was working perfectly. I calmly enjoyed my juice and cookie while imagining the wonder the congregation was about to behold.

"Thaddeus, you've done it again," I thought to myself. "Another improvement accomplished."

A Thaddeus Fun Fact

Thomas Edison had 1,093 patents in his lifetime, a number I plan on passing by the time I'm twenty. I also plan to bench press up to 250 pounds, be able to dunk a basketball, and have named at least thirty new spider species. Mrs. Garza says if you don't write down your goals, they're just dreams. I have now officially made them goals.

Just before the service, I took my acolyte robe out of its special drawer and lit my walnut-handled, brass candle lighting stick (which I am sure has a more specific name, probably Latin in nature, but I can't find it and Pastor Snodgrass has not been helpful in the least with this information. The research will continue).

I then located the everyday, cheapo lighter that Pastor Snodgrass keeps in the desk in the alcove outside of the sanctuary. Actually, this was one of my suggestions for him. Why not get a more ceremonial lighting instrument? It seems to me that using a lighter from a gas station designed for lighting cigarettes is not the message we should be giving the congregation. He claimed that no one ever saw the lighter, so why did it really matter? So, the good Lord doesn't care how his candle is lit? Oh, really?

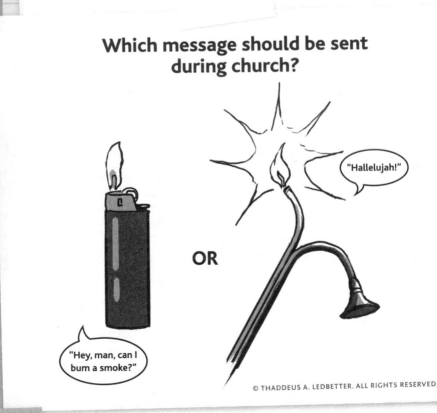

With an attitude like this, how this man became an ordained minister is beyond me. Do you adults just have to fill out some paperwork to get these positions?

Still, he has his good points, and I'm sure that he would enjoy the increase in attendance. The ringing of the hour occurred to start the service, and we started the procession down the center aisle toward the pulpit. I was almost shaking with excitement for what was about to happen.

A Thaddeus Fun Fact (Church Edition)

The word "cemetery" actually comes from the Greek word *koimeterion*, meaning "sleeping place, dormitory." I'm thinking this represents the idea of death as sleep, not that a grave is a good place for a nap. Though when I am in a cemetery, I'm usually not feeling sleepy.

RIP

Zzzzzzz

I had shaved off the top one-eighth of an inch of the sparkly part of the sparkler, leaving just the wick part exposed, to make it easier to light. So when I lit the candle and moved on, it looked the same as usual.

But this is where circumstances I couldn't control come into play. Just as Pastor Snodgrass was passing the altar, as luck would have it, the sparkler began sparkling. REALLY sparkling!

I think when I was scraping down the sparkler for lighting ease, I may have concentrated the potassium chlorate (the active ingredient in sparklers) down the wick, and when the flame got there, it made this really huge, very cool, sparkle.

DEFENSE

That's when the sparkler met Pastor Snodgrass's preaching robe. Due to his proximity, the sparkler kind of set his robe on fire.

Now, the first second or two, it was just sparking. But I'm thinking that the preaching-robe industry is not under the same stringent flame-retardant regulations of children's pajamas, because the robe went up in flames quickly! Unfortunately, Pastor Snodgrass did not react appropriately.

THADDEUS A. LEDBETTER
DEFENSE

So here's the situation: Pastor Snodgrass is standing there in front of the obviously stunned congregation as his robe goes up in flames. Luckily, he has a suit, a suit that must have been certified fire safe by OSHA, which is keeping the actual flames from his person. Still, the man's standing there on fire.

STOP

How does one react when on fire? Stop, drop, and roll! I thought everyone knew this.

DROP

and ROLL!

DEFENSE

Seeing that he is stunned or in shock, just standing there like a big Fourth of July Roman candle, I instinctually do the practical thing and resort to my Boy Scout training. I started shouting, "Stop, drop, and roll!!!! Stop, drop, and roll, man!!"

Could I have been any clearer? But get this—Pastor Snodgrass neither stopped, dropped, nor rolled. What's up with that? It had only been a couple of seconds, but I could tell this might get dangerous. If he wasn't going to do any dropping and rolling, someone had to do something.

That someone was me.

Springing into action, I grabbed the first fire-extinguishing tool I could locate, the large, fire-smothering material I saw hanging from the pulpit. I grabbed it, rushed over, wrapped it around him, and then tackled the pastor to the ground, repeatedly beating him with the material and smothering the flames until they were out.

Yes, you read that correctly. I saved Pastor Snodgrass from a fiery death.

When everyone calmed down and we were sure Pastor Snodgrass was no longer in danger, was I celebrated? No. Did a rousing round of handshakes and "well-dones" commence? Not even close. Even worse, everyone started yelling at me. Again with the yelling. That material I had used to save the pastor's life turned out to be the vestments, or "special hangings" of the church. Yes, they are special and blessed and represent the sanctity of the service, but what can you do? I had to put the man out.

So I save a man's life, the leader of a church no less, and the thanks I get? Accused of sabotaging a church service and endangering the life of a man of the cloth.

The level of injustice is overwhelming. This one lifesaving occurrence alone should be enough to get me out of In-School Suspension. I understand if you feel bad for perpetuating such a grand injustice.

I patiently await your response.

Thaddeus

A Thaddeus Fun Fact
(School Edition)

This one is specifically designed for your edification, Mr. Cooper. Since I am so good at increasing attendance at church, I can use my skills in helping you increase attendance at school.

Isn't it against the law not to go to school? And yet you have attendance problems? Wow, that's hard to do. Good job.

But if you are trying to increase attendance, your previous attempts have been laughable at best: perfect attendance for a week and we get a pencil! Wow, can't wait to sharpen this bad boy! (Sarcasm should be evident.) And perfect attendance for the semester merits a certificate with the principal's photocopied signature on it! No way! (Again, please note sarcasm.)

If you truly want to increase attendance rates, here's how you do it. It's the old theme-restaurant approach to increasing traffic.

- **Refer-to-your-teachers-by-their-first-names Mondays:**
  You would not believe how worked up teachers get if you call them by their first names. I probably have half a dozen write-ups just for this alone. What's the big deal? Aren't we all humans, here? If on Monday, I can say, "Here's my homework, Priscilla," aren't we all better for it?

- **Flip-your-grade Tuesdays:**
  If you get a 39% on your pop quiz, you can flip it to a 93%. It makes things more interesting.

- **Quiz-free Wednesdays:**

  If I know that a teacher isn't going to give a vindictive quiz just because I was too busy to do her reading the night before, I'm much more likely to show up to school.

- **In-the-ballpark Thursdays:**

  The teacher asks a question—say, something about a president—and you name an actual president, you get credit for "being in the ballpark." It wouldn't help students like me who always get the answer exactly right, but it will encourage the attendance of troglodytes like Billy Cunningham.

- **Open-phone Fridays:**

  This one is based on those radio talk shows that open up certain topics for their listeners. The teachers let the students decide what the material covered will be, and open up the floor to suggestions, opinions, and general comments. I guarantee I would never miss a Friday if this were implemented.

There you go. Excluding Ebola virus outbreaks or an attack of influenza-laced swine, you can pretty much expect perfect attendance every day if you use my suggestions.

PRISON JOURNAL, CONTINUED

DAY 23:

- The kids and Mrs. Garza have been doing my improved Pledge of Allegiance, so I sent a new one that reflects my new circumstances. Maybe a daily, public declaration of the injustice against me will help my cause.
- Nachos for lunch.

DAY 24:

- Absent.

DAY 25:

- I didn't have to go to school yesterday. My mom and I went to my dad's grave. It was my dad's birthday. She told me that he would have been proud of me, though he wouldn't like me being in so much trouble. For the millionth time, I tried to explain how it wasn't my fault.
- Then she said, "There is definitely a lot of your father in you. I remember how he always drove me crazy with some of his ideas. But it was also kind of endearing. When we were dating, I remember he would plan our dates to the minute because he didn't want to waste a minute of valuable courting time."
- I'm not exactly sure what that means, but my father was obviously a very intelligent man. I know he could really help me with my defense.

DAY 26:

- Been very busy today. Did some math, English, and wrote an extra-credit report on spiders that I'm submitting to the national spider registry.

- Mrs. Calhoun says Shirley says hi. I said hi back.
- Nachos for lunch.

DAY 27:

- Again, very busy. Mrs. Dixon even came and got me to help her unload her car for the diorama project. How one makes dioramas for math I have no idea. I suspect it just wastes a lot of class time so she doesn't have to teach.
- She had like a million shoe boxes, cotton balls, and bottle cleaners in the trunk of her car. And when I said, "Wow, Mrs. Dixon, you've got a lot of junk in your trunk," Mr. Wilson, the janitor who was also helping, laughed, and Mrs. Dixon got all mad. Weird. She takes her trunk very seriously.
- Nachos for lunch.

DAY 28:

- Got a great idea for a new blues song and spent most of the day writing it. I may have enough songs for an album pretty soon. I need to get a black-and-white picture of myself looking sad, standing in the rain, and wearing a cool hat.

DAY 29:

- It was the field trip to the science museum today, and I didn't get to go. Mr. Hardy also kicked me out of the Scouts. Yeah, life's real fair.

DAY 30:

- Nothing.

DAY 31:

- I really don't feel like doing anything today, either. My mom wasn't upset that I was kicked out of the Boy Scouts. She says we really can't afford the time or money. Maybe I'll get a job. Someone with my talents has to be highly marketable. I bet I can get a special provision waiving child labor restrictions. I wish I hadn't been "ruled out" of making presentations to the city council.

DAY 32:

- Wrote Billy's paper today. At least I know he's my enemy, unlike those other two-faced snakes. Based the whole thing on Dolly Madison being great at making snack cakes. Since I was able to work in all the dumb things he says, neither he nor anyone else will know the difference.

- Since some of the kids have started a petition to get me out of ISS, I probably should send them some suggestions on how to get the most signatures quickly. Finally, someone realizes how important I am to this school!

- Nachos for lunch.

DAY 33:

- There are rumblings among the students about how damaging it is not having me around and not being able to help out our school. I knew it would happen eventually. Now if I can just get Mr. Cooper to read my defense and listen to the people. This is a democracy, right?

- Had two trays of nachos for lunch and Shirley sent me some brownies. This day was SOOOO LIVE.

Billy Cunningham

Mrs. Garza

American History

A report about Dolly Madison

Dolly Madison was this old lady who lived a long time ago. She did lots of things for those guys who were the first presidents, like George Washington and Benjamin Franklin. For example, she made them the following snacks:

- lemon pies
- chocolate pies
- cherry pies
- pies with that creamy white stuff no one knows what to call

She also did other cool things like:

- named the second-place arm wrestling champ at the Constitutional Convention
- punched that king guy from England in the throat
- killed a bear with her bare hands
- Won a mixed martial arts title

In conclusion, Dolly Madison was a woman. She liked to bake delicious pies. She could kick your butt. And that is why the United States is so great today.

Written by Billy "Mixed Martial Arts Champ" Cunningham.

Thaddeus,

Thank you so much for patiently awaiting my response. As you can see, you are not the only one who can use sarcasm.

And as a matter of fact, setting your pastor on fire is not a reason for positive recognition. You're lucky that Pastor Snodgrass was not seriously injured. I just hope you haven't totally destroyed the mentor program.

Also, the district has finally settled the suit brought by Mr. Dunham. One of the stipulations is that you provide a public apology, so start working on that.

You might also be surprised to know, as I was, that several of your classmates are asking for you to be released from ISS. It's not going to happen.

Mr. Cooper

THE OVERLY
SENSITIVE ARTISTS

Discipline Referral Form

Student's Name: _Thaddeus Ledbetter_ Grade: _7_ Gender: _M_

Teacher's Name: _____

Location of Offense: _CCMS library_

Reason(s) for Referral

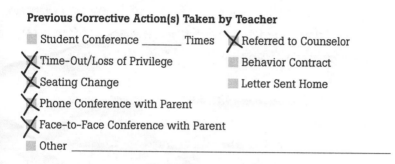

He tried to destroy our careers!

Previous Corrective Action(s) Taken by Teacher

- ☐ Student Conference _____ Times
- ☒ Time-Out/Loss of Privilege
- ☒ Seating Change
- ☒ Phone Conference with Parent
- ☒ Face-to-Face Conference with Parent
- ☐ Other _____
- ☒ Referred to Counselor
- ☐ Behavior Contract
- ☐ Letter Sent Home

Action(s) Taken by Administrator

- ☐ Discussion
- ☒ Warning/Probation
- ☐ Student Conference
- ☐ Contacted Parent
- ☐ Detention
- ☐ D.A.E.P. Assignment
- ☐ Other _____
- ☐ Verbal Reprimand
- ☐ Referred to Counselor
- ☐ Detention
- ☐ In-School Suspension (ISS)
- ☐ Expulsion
- ☐ Referral to Law Enforcement

Administrator Signature _Principal Frank Cooper_

Student Signature _Thaddeus A. Ledbetter (soon to be Esq.)_

<u>2/12</u> Thaddeus has been sending me a very detailed "defense" of his actions, incident-by-incident, for several weeks now. If he would just put this much effort into his work, he would be a straight-A student.

<u>2/20</u> Several students have approached me about Thaddeus's punishment, and surprisingly, not in appreciation. For a kid who annoyed so much of the student body, I can't believe they want him back in class. Some are saying the teachers act differently when Thaddeus isn't around. Surely this can't be true.

<u>3/11</u> Just had a meeting with Mrs. Ledbetter, Thaddeus's mother. This is the first time I've met with her since Thaddeus was placed in ISS. She wanted me to know some "mitigating" details about Thaddeus and his situation (apparently he treats her to his "Fun Facts" also). Some things do explain a few of his idiosyncrasies:

1) Mr. Ledbetter passed away a little over a year ago from cancer. Mrs. Ledbetter believes Thaddeus is dealing with this loss by constantly trying to "improve" other things in his life. The timing does coincide with the increased intensity of Thaddeus's need for "improvements."

2) Thaddeus's father was an efficiency expert by profession, and he seemed to try to live his life with this approach, too. His motto was "work smarter, not harder," and he ingrained this into Thaddeus. Mrs. Ledbetter says that Thaddeus

takes pride in the fact that "no one works less hard than him."
I'm not sure what that means, or if it's a good thing.

3) Furthermore, Thaddeus's dad believed that helping people
be more efficient was the noblest of callings because it
made people's lives better. He instilled this philosophy in
his son, maybe a little too much. I guess that explains all
the notes in the suggestion box.

4) Mrs. Ledbetter thinks that even though Thaddeus is
trying to stay strong and be the man of the house, his
father's birthday really hit him hard this year.

5) Thaddeus seems to also be preoccupied with "preparing
for any contingency." His mother thinks that this is a
reaction to the powerlessness he, and everyone, feels
when watching a loved one battle a horrible disease. I
got the impression his mother thinks Thaddeus blames
himself for not being able to help his father more, so
now he is obsessed with never being caught in a helpless
situation again. This makes his "true emergency drill" a
bit more comprehensible. I've scheduled a meeting with his
counselor, Mrs. Hamm, to discuss strategies in dealing with
Thaddeus's need to prepare for everything.

This information definitely helps me understand Thaddeus
better, but it still doesn't release him from ISS. I will try
to keep this in mind when dealing with him, but even after
hearing Mrs. Ledbetter's concerns, I still believe his ISS
placement is the best for everyone involved.

A Heart-Healthy Parking Plan

Mr. Cooper, you could greatly help your staff with a system based on the BMI (Body Mass Index). Obesity causes heart disease, diabetes, and even cancer, so you're only helping these chubs by having them walk a little bit.

Assign parking spots according to the teachers' BMIs. Those in shape will stay in shape to keep their good spots, and the fatties will inevitably lose weight from the longer walk.

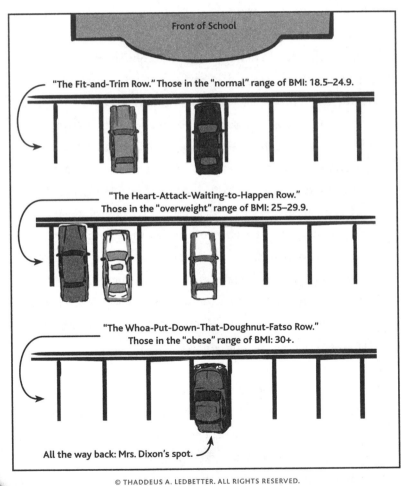

Front of School

"The Fit-and-Trim Row." Those in the "normal" range of BMI: 18.5–24.9.

"The Heart-Attack-Waiting-to-Happen Row." Those in the "overweight" range of BMI: 25–29.9.

"The Whoa-Put-Down-That-Doughnut-Fatso Row." Those in the "obese" range of BMI: 30+.

All the way back: Mrs. Dixon's spot.

THADDEUS A. LEDBETTER
DEFENSE

Mr. Cooper,

I'm still in detention, so I'm assuming, though you claim to have read my defense, that you are either not reading it closely or you're not getting all the accompanying paperwork.

Not to tell you how to do your job, but you seem to have a problem with your systems when it comes to receiving my communiqués. I'd be happy to look over your responsibility flow-chart and locate areas of improvement. I'm real good at that, an amateur efficiency expert if you will.

Furthermore, I must repeat, I don't see how an occurrence at church has anything to do with school at all. Why was Pastor Snodgrass at the discipline meeting anyway? All that yelling didn't seem appropriate for a man of the cloth. This had nothing to do with the mentoring program.

Now, this next supposed "incident" did take place within your jurisdiction, namely the school library. But if you had been there, you would have noticed that the so-called adult presenters were the ones who started all the trouble.

A Thaddeus Fun Fact

The word "hysteria" comes from the Greek word *hysterikos*, meaning . . . whoa, I can't write about this. It's about body parts that really shouldn't be discussed in public. You know, those of a feminine persuasion. This makes me uncomfortable. Look it up yourself if you're so interested, weirdo.

. . . .

PERCEIVED DISCIPLINARY ACCUSATION #4:

Ruining Mrs. West's, the librarian's, fine-arts program, and possibly destroying its reputation with all future performers.

ACTUAL EVENT:

Pointing out the obvious and saving the world from more nonsense with some constructive criticism.

. . . .

This misunderstanding took place during one of Mrs. West's "special presentations to expose the students to knowledge outside of the curriculum," an idea I think is great. Though I think her choices have been a bit questionable.

We could have been enlightened by an arachnologist, lexicographer, computer programmer, or if we really wanted to learn about music, how about a bluesman? No, instead we get a lot of puppeteers and mimes. I'm not sure how pretending to be in an invisible box is a marketable skill, but as far as useless skills go, that guy was really good.

Still, I don't think that "walking into the pretend wind with a pretend umbrella" is going to get you into Harvard or MIT, but I humored them.

But this last time, Mrs. West pushed the uselessness too far with her "A Singer, a Poet, and a Painter, Oh My!" presentation. I think that's supposed to be a reference to a children's song or something. Of course, they didn't explain the reference. That would have been too informative for this bunch.

Now for the other presentations, I didn't mind missing classes like history or speech. (On that subject: speech? Is this class really necessary? I'm fairly certain most seventh-graders know how to vibrate their vocal cords to produce the noise we refer to as "speech." What a waste of valuable class time. How about adding a course in Japanese for us anime fans? Or maybe something on deep-space astronomy? Even better, spiders. I mean, who with half a brain doesn't love spiders? The possibilities are endless, yet we have a class devoted to a basic human function. You might want to bring this up with the curriculum director.)

THADDEUS A. LEDBETTER
DEFENSE

Crooked Creek's Guide to Worthless Courses

SLEEPING 101: The teacher will turn off the lights, play some soft music (or a recording of Mr. Cooper's morning announcements), and instruct students to close their eyes.

DIGESTING FOR BEGINNERS: Students will ingest various foods and let their bodies get sustenance. Prerequisites: Chewing 201 and Advanced Swallowing.

MIMING 112: Learn how to pull a pretend rope, be boxed up in a pretend box, and pretend other things for no apparent reason.

SPEECH: See regular course guide.

But for this needless presentation, Mrs. West chose third period, when I happen to have a useful course, computer science. Here I am, having finished all my assigned work, despite what Mr. Collins says about all his extra busywork that has nothing to do with actual computing, and I'm just about to finish my program that would make the cafeteria line go much more quickly (it involves moving those students who are purchasing nachos to the front of the line—I call it the "Nacho Flash Pass"), and we get called down to the library.

The Food Pyramid that finally presents the accurate consumption of the lunches served at Crooked Creek Middle School by the student body, and the order in which students should be served.

Note, those at the top of the pyramid will be served first, those at the bottom, last.

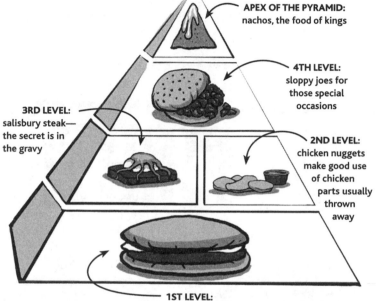

APEX OF THE PYRAMID: nachos, the food of kings

4TH LEVEL: sloppy joes for those special occasions

3RD LEVEL: salisbury steak—the secret is in the gravy

2ND LEVEL: chicken nuggets make good use of chicken parts usually thrown away

1ST LEVEL: hamburger/cheeseburger—staple eaten daily by entire student body

As we walked down the hall, I couldn't help but notice how quickly we progressed through the empty halls, reinforcing the need for my important-student lane (please see earlier missive). When we got to the library, I had my hopes up that maybe the special presentation would be the guy from the zoo. He sometimes brings a tarantula to presentations, and though it is nowhere near as poisonous as the brown recluse, it at least looks cool.

THADDEUS A. LEDBETTER
DEFENSE

(I wonder what would happen if a brown recluse and a tarantula fought. While the tarantula would definitely have a size and weight advantage, the recluse is cagey and crafty. I'd find out, but I figure the animal-rights folks would be all over me. The last thing I need right now are a bunch of picketers bringing more attention to me. My uncle Pete would freak out over that kind of coverage. But a Spider Royale Cage Match would be cool.)

But no such luck with the zoo guy. It was the "Singer, a Poet, and a Painter, Oh My!" presentation, though a better name for it would be "Senseless Things People Who Can't Get Real Jobs Do." It's my understanding Mrs. West videotaped the performance, but I don't think a videotape can accurately capture just how bad these presentations were.

Wait, that's right! You have a tape of the presentation! You have a record of my comments and the unwarranted responses to them. How is this even an issue anymore? Check the tape!

The video was shot from behind us, and if you don't recognize the back of my head, you can identify me as the one quietly holding up my hand most of the time.

And what's the deal with that? During your whole school career, you're trained to raise your hand if you have a question or comment. Yet by the third day of class, even if I am raising my hand, the teacher doesn't ever call on me. So at this dumb arts presentation, after my second comment, the teacher stopped calling on me even though my hand was up the whole time. I'm playing by the rules, so why aren't you grown-ups? Maybe I could be issued a bell or buzzer since this hand-raising thing isn't working.

A Thaddeus Fun Fact

While raising the hand is the cheapest and oldest way for a student to request to be acknowledged, we could really improve response time by implementing signals used in other areas of life, including but not limited to: Naval signal flags, air horns used at sporting events, game-show buzzers, track meet start pistols (it would keep the teachers on their toes if they knew the next time they asked an easy question, there would be a barrage of gunfire).

YOU ARE SO DEAD!!!! What was that crap you gave me? Not only did I fail, but Mrs. Garza made me read it in front of the class!!

And they laughed at me!!!!

So I've spent the afternoon beating up all those little punks who thought they could laugh at me and get away with it.

But I'm saving the bone-crunching, snot-spitting, face-breaking beating for you.

Billy "Your Death Sentence" Cunningham

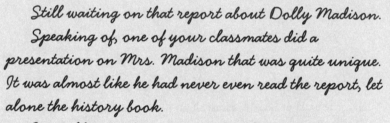

Thaddeus,

Still waiting on that report about Dolly Madison.

Speaking of, one of your classmates did a presentation on Mrs. Madison that was quite unique. It was almost like he had never even read the report, let alone the history book.

I would go as far as saying it felt as if this student made or paid another student to do it for him. We all know that providing work for other students is still considered cheating.

Mrs. Garza

P.S. Nicely done.
P.P.S. The kids are passing something around about you—you're not getting them in trouble, are you?
P.P.P.S. I still need to check your notebook.

DEFENSE

Really, don't these people have parents, or at least friends?
Does the phrase "marketable skill" ever come up when people talk
to them?

And you should know that I have made it my life's calling
to help people do the things they do better and to work smarter,
not harder. Anyone who works really hard at what they do is just
wasting their time. And so I just give them some suggestions. And
all the evidence supports this.

Somehow, based on your lack of school-improvement
implementations, I have the feeling you haven't combed over my
transcripts of the event, noting the context of my comments. Let's
hit the highlights.

You'll notice that I did not "question the integrity of their
art." (Are all so-called artists this sensitive?) I actually gave
some constructive criticism. I believe they call it "notes" in show
business, at least from the movies I've seen.

Please also note that I quietly sat through each of their performances, politely raised my hand throughout, and emphatically waved only after they were through. I waited to be acknowledged (though the painter seemed to be a bit hesitant), and only then did I give my notes for improvement. I had already lost my computer time, so I thought I might as well get something productive done by improving the arts.

As luck would have it, I saved my notes. Actually, it wasn't luck. I keep rigorous records and notes of all my activities for the benefit of future historians. But please note that most are in the form of questions, which shouldn't be the least bit offensive. This is exactly what I read to the presenters, as well as some mitigating information that I have since added. Please see attached.

And understand that I read my notes verbatim to the presenters. What's so offensive?

Thaddeus Fun Facts

The word "verbatim" comes from the Latin word *verbum*, meaning "word." So technically, that last sentence has terms for the word "word" five times. That may be a record. I may need to start keeping a tally on thaddeus-ledbetter.com.

• • •

"Folk" comes from the German *volk*. Apparently, these common people enjoyed songs about dumb things and really liked hammering and trying to beat a steam-powered drilling machine in tunneling through a mountain.

Notes for Eddie Fitzgerald – Folk Singer

1. Are suspenders really a good fashion idea? Doesn't that kind of send the message of "I can't make enough money from my music to afford a belt"?

   I remember my dad telling my uncle once when he was wearing suspenders that unless he worked at Ye Olde Country Store and his name was "Uncle Charlie," he looked ridiculous.

2. Your guitar playing seems limited to only three chords. Have you thought about some lessons? Or changing to the blues? They only use two chords, and it is a vastly superior form of music (I even have some songs I can sell you).

   After thinking about it, this guy was way too happy to really capture the blues. (Not to mention the rainbow suspenders.)

3. Why are you encouraging us to always sing along? Isn't it your job as the professional to handle the singing?

   Do comedians ask you to tell jokes at their shows?
   Boxers want you to take a few punches for them?
   How are singers getting away with this?

4. Have you actually listened to the lyrics you're singing? Like that hammer song in which you discuss using your hammer for the entire day across what sounds like a very large area. Are you just hammering willy-nilly? Doing unsolicited hammering at people's houses and places of business? Is this some sort of obsessive-compulsive disorder? Most people wouldn't think mental disorders make good song lyrics. Have you thought this out?

   Have you noticed how a lot of folk songs don't make a lot of sense? Lots of boat rowing, cotton picking, and identification of land ownership with dubious legal support. Not sure these subjects are really song-worthy.

5. Do you know any classical guitar? You ought to study that if you're going to be hardheaded about not playing the blues. At least that's a real talent.

6. Do you still live with your parents? I get the feeling you do. Turns out I was right, and I think it touched a nerve. Maybe if he lost the suspenders he could get a real job.

Notes for Agatha Simmons – Children's Poet

1. Do you realize most of your poems don't rhyme? Are you just not good at rhyming? You know there's a rhyming dictionary here in the library, not to mention all of the ones online.

   If you think about it, is rhyming really too much to ask for in your poetry? Otherwise, it's just regular talking.

2. That sure was a long poem about how wonderful and squishy mud is. Maybe things have changed since you were a kid, but kids really aren't into mud anymore.

   Do you adults have any idea what kids like and dislike? Really? Mud? Come on, despite what you think, we're not fascinated with filth.

3. Are some of your poems supposed to be funny? You seemed to pause for us to laugh, but not many people laughed, except for the teachers, and they seemed to be forcing it.

   This was really uncomfortable.

4. In one of your poems, you have a tiger talking to a monkey. I can guarantee, even if it was a talking monkey, the moment a tiger saw the monkey, the tiger would devour it. Though that probably wouldn't make a very good children's poem. *Obviously, this lady has never seen the Nature Channel.*

5. Do you have any poems about serious subjects? You have a lot about pretending to be sick to miss school, getting a bad haircut, and ice cream, but you know, we kids do have some serious concerns. Like the plight of the endangered green soft-shell turtle, for instance. You should write a poem about that. You can go to my Web site, thaddeus-ledbetter.com, to find out more about it and how I'm doing my part to save the turtle.

Finally, is it true no word rhymes with "orange"?
Geesh, look whom I'm asking!

THADDEUS A. LEDBETTER
DEFENSE

> ### A Thaddeus Fun Fact
> Contrary to popular belief, the word "purple" does have a rhyme: "slurple."
> As in, "My soup is so good I just have to slurple it up." I personally use it all
> the time. I also like the word "kumquat." A lot of people think it's made up,
> but it's a real word.

For a poet who spent so much time talking about laughter and
happiness, she sure got all moody and sad. Chrissy Nichols
claims she heard Mrs. Simmons crying afterward and that it was
all my fault. That's ridiculous. She probably just has allergies or
something. You read the comments—what was cry-worthy?
The last presenter was local artist Charles McCurdy, who will
remain "local" if he doesn't take my advice. He claims he is an
"abstract expressionist." If you have read my defense of the "Slug
Bug Incident" (which I doubt you did, because I am still in ISS),
you know that I have definitively proven that this is not an actual
art form. What is an "abstract expressionist," you ask? Please see
Fun Fact.

> ### A Thaddeus Fun Fact
> Abstract expressionism gets its name from "abstract," from the Latin
> *abstractus,* meaning "drawn away from," and "express," from the Latin
> *expressus,* meaning "clearly presented." Thus when put together, you
> get "drawn away from the clearly presented." In other words, trying
> not to make sense. When it comes to pointless nonsense, the abstract
> expressionist is a master.

Notes for Charles McCurdy – Abstract Expressionist Artist

1. You talked a lot about letting your emotions out on the canvas. Just what emotions are you talking about? Messiness? Confusion? A feeling of pointlessness?

   You could also add "poor spatial relationship," "poor eyesight," maybe even "mental impairment," but I respectfully left those off the list.

2. Why do you bother to give your paintings titles? Your painting "Happiness in the Modern World" is just a bunch of yellow, black, blue, and orange lines. How does that indicate happiness? Maybe you could include a happy face or a clown.

   I'm not sure Mr. McCurdy has a good grip on the English language.

3. Have you thought about painting dogs doing human things? My uncle Pete has this great painting of dogs playing poker. You'd probably sell a lot more if you had dogs doing things like playing charades, having a political debate, or starting a small business.

   People love dogs.

4. How much do you get for your paintings? I saw a show
   where paintings by a monkey, an elephant, and a cat were
   selling for more than $5,000. Surely you get more than
   $5,000, since you are a human artist and everything.

   How can this be considered rude? I thought it was a given that a
   human would make more than a monkey. Or a cat? C'mon.

THADDEUS A. LEDBETTER
DEFENSE

I'm not sure when they turned off the video recorder, but it was just after I asked if he made more than a monkey that Mr. McCurdy shouted, "I've wasted my life!" and stormed out of the library, just leaving all of his stuff there.

I guess he's one of those sensitive-artist types, but is that really my fault? Those paintings are probably still in the library if you want them, though I have no idea why you would.

Well, that's that. I'm really not sure how I can make this any clearer. Again, I suspect you are not closely reading all of my reports. Which leads me to another efficiency suggestion.

My dad's motto was "Work smarter, not harder," and I have turned it into a personal goal to never work hard. Yet look at all the work I get done. Yes, I know this is impressive.

I'll let you in on a secret, and then you can implement it across the campus. The secret is to only do the important work, especially when it comes to paperwork, reports, and such. For example, Dolly Madison has been fully explored. No need for me to waste more paper doing it.

But I have noticed that almost all of my teachers complain about having to turn in lesson plans both at the beginning of the day and the end of day. Something about documenting what was planned and what was accomplished. Well, I can tell you what is NOT being accomplished: reading my suggestions and then implementing them in our classes.

I'm thinking that these reports must be eating up a lot of your time, too, Mr. Cooper. Here's my efficiency suggestion: Lose the daily reports. Let's get the teachers focusing on what's important, which is me and some of the other kids (read: the smart ones). I've gotten the impression that the teachers feel the same way, but are afraid to tell you. I'm not. I remember back in fifth grade, when you came over to my elementary school for a "Going to Middle School" orientation (if you recall, I was the one who asked about your dog policy and recommended the junior administrator policy board), you said that you were always open to suggestions for school improvement.

And just think, when I get out of ISS, I can get you these suggestions even more quickly.

A Thaddeus Fun Fact
(Education Edition)

There is a direct correlation between the decrease in lesson-plan writing and the increase of standardized test scores. I'll cite my source later, but you can bet it's a good one. Also, free nachos seem to increase scores. And free sodas.

PRISON JOURNAL, CONTINUED

DAY 34:

- We finally went back to church yesterday and my mom said it wasn't too bad, though some of those old ladies in the back need to mind their own business.
- Pastor Snodgrass wouldn't let me be the candle-lighting acolyte, though. The new kid doing it was awful. His steps down the aisle were all out of tempo, he was wearing white socks, and one of the candles even blew out when he turned around too quickly. Surely everyone has noticed the mistakes since I stopped being the acolyte.
- Got an interesting note from Mrs. Garza, but I may have to avoid Billy for a while.
- Nachos for lunch.

DAY 35:

- Mrs. Calhoun brought me one of those boy-wizard-at-magic-school books that are all the rage. I really don't get it. Doesn't everyone realize that if you're in a world where everyone could shift shapes, listen through walls, and magically turn into a bug, you would be so paranoid that life would be miserable? You would never be sure you're talking to your friend—maybe it's a bad guy who looks like your friend, or just a regular ant. Folks would go insane in, like, a week. And their school has constantly moving staircases. How would you control traffic patterns if you didn't know where a staircase was going to be? It's just dumb. Why was I given this book to read?

- Have a bad feeling about Billy. Having my mom drop me off instead of taking the bus.
- Just to get away from that stupid wizard book, did a little work on Mrs. Garza's Dolly Madison paper.

DAY 36:

- Have found out some interesting facts about Dolly Madison. Like when the British were burning down the White House during the War of 1812, which took place in 1812 as the name would indicate (if all wars were named this efficiently, it sure would cut down the amount of time to learn history facts), she saved many of the paintings. I guess this is cool, but a bucket of water might have been more helpful. May get a Fun Fact from all this.

DAY 37:

- Working on my defense against those really sensitive artistic folks who can't handle a little constructive criticism. It would probably help their careers if they implemented my suggestions.
- The more I think about it, the more I don't get the artistic kind. They're always spouting about searching for "truth," yet you give them a little truth and they all freak out.
- Luckily, I kept a copy of my performance notes that I gave them, so that should be all the documentation I need to prove I was not in the wrong. I'm impressed how insightful the notes are.
- Nachos for lunch.

DAY 38:

- Still working on this artistic defense. See Mrs. West's videotape for evidence. I wonder if shaky librarian footage of a dozen snotty kids making sniffing noises in the background would be admissible in court.

- E-mailed Uncle Pete about the librarian footage. Hopefully, I will get a reply soon.

- Mrs. Calhoun says Shirley loves those dumb wizard-in-magic-school books. (The books are dumb, not the wizard, though I'm not so sure now that I think about it. How would you not just charm yourself straight A's if you had any sense?) Shirley may know her baked goods and fiber needs, but she doesn't know anything about literature.

DAY 39:

- Submitted full defense to Mr. Cooper via Mrs. Calhoun. I wonder if that is a problem. Maybe she got confused and delivered it to the gym or something. Maybe I should get a receipt.

- Really hope he lets me out. I'm really tired today. I think I'm tired from being stuck in here, bored out of my mind. That, and always being strong for my mom.

- Mrs. Calhoun let me take a nap all afternoon. She even let me borrow her pillow.

Thaddeus,

I assure you again, I read your defenses, every word, even
the painful ones, that you have submitted to me. I even
have a file I keep them in, though usually for legal reasons.
But I have recently reread your file with all your numerous
defenses, suggestions, and all the other correspondence you
have blessed me with.

And when I read them, I must admit, you do make some
valid points.

However, Thaddeus, your life could be so much easier
and more productive if you would just change your tone.
Sometimes it's not what you say but how you say it.

But you mentioned that the teachers were spending
too much time on their daily lesson plans and it was
becoming detrimental to the learning process. No one
had mentioned it to me, but at the last faculty meeting,
I brought the subject up. One of the teachers felt
comfortable to voice her true opinions, and I was
surprised to find the entire faculty was unanimous in
their professional opinions that our lesson-plan system was
causing more harm than good.

So I have modified the lesson-plan cycle to a weekly
form, and the staff seems very pleased. I even mentioned
to the staff that you had made this suggestion. It was
clear that even though you have been removed from the

student body for over a month, you have in no way been forgotten.

But you need to be responsible for your actions, because I am still dealing with the very serious ramifications of your very dangerous drill, so I believe a yearlong In-School Suspension is appropriate.

Mr. Cooper

THE TRUE EMERGENCY
DRILL

Discipline Referral Form

Student's Name: _Thaddeus Ledbetter_   Grade: _7_   Gender: _M_

Teacher's Name: _____

Location of Offense: _CCMS_

Reason(s) for Referral

THIS KID IS A MENACE!!!

Previous Corrective Action(s) Taken by Teacher

- ☐ Student Conference _____ Times
- ☒ Time-Out/Loss of Privilege
- ☒ Seating Change
- ☒ Phone Conference with Parent
- ☒ Face-to-Face Conference with Parent
- ☐ Other _____
- ☒ Referred to Counselor
- ☐ Behavior Contract
- ☒ Letter Sent Home

Action(s) Taken by Administrator

- ☒ Discussion
- ☒ Warning/Probation
- ☐ Student Conference
- ☒ Contacted Parent
- ☐ Detention
- ☐ D.A.E.P. Assignment
- ☐ Other _____
- ☒ Verbal Reprimand
- ☒ Referred to Counselor
- ☐ Detention
- ☐ In-School Suspension (ISS)
- ☐ Expulsion
- ☐ Referral to Law Enforcement

Administrator Signature _Principal Frank Cooper_

Student Signature _Thaddeus A. Ledbetter (soon to be Esq.)_

Crooked Creek
CHURCH

Welcoming of worshipers, voicing of congregation news

First Hymn #1,533: "To Forgive Is Divine"

Invocation and Calling to Confession

Scripture readings

Sermon: "How even fire cannot destroy love"
(or "Welcoming back the prodigal acolyte").
An exploration of the spiritual need to forgive *everyone*, even
if they set you on fire. By Pastor Lawrence Snodgrass

Second Hymn: #1,128: "Three Young Men in a Furnace."
The story of Shadrach, Meshach, and Abednego and their
faith through fire.

Collection of tithes and offerings
(Please welcome our new plate bearer, Thaddeus Ledbetter,
in his new, safer role in the service.)

Crooked Creek
CHURCH

GUEST BOOK

Pastor Snodgrass,

I took you up on your offer and attended your
service this week. Though I enjoyed the fellowship
and singing, I suspect your invitation was not out
of concern for the well-being of my soul.

  Actually, I wonder if the choice of hymns and
sermon was for my benefit. I am glad that you
have the grace to forgive Thaddeus for his "help"
(and while it was dangerous, I don't think it was
malicious). I don't have that luxury. I have a whole
school to think about.

Nice try,
Frank Cooper (Principal, CCMS)

Thaddy My Boy,

Why are you using the librarian's videotape for your defense? I'm not sure it's relevant anymore.

I had some friends here at the firm looking at the charges against you regarding your True Emergency Drill. Technically, you could be in a lot of serious, serious trouble. But I think if we can put things in context, really play up how your motivation was to help, and point out that no one was actually harmed during your drill, we may be able to get you out of ISS.

Your best bet is to just lay low and stay quiet until this thing blows over. I also know that this is like asking a fish not to swim, but can you please try?

So if you have to keep making your defense, please do so with as little incriminating information as possible. And maybe be a little nicer to Mr. Cooper?

I think we're going to pull your butt out of the fire
on this one, so don't mess it up.

Uncle Pete

Thaddeus,

Everyone is talking about you, and I mean
everyone! Like a million people have signed the
petition to get you out of ISS, and even some of
the teachers are saying it's unfair.

There were a couple of kids with homemade
"Free Thaddeus" shirts on today, and everyone is
talking about going home and making them.

It is soooooooo cool! How can Mr. Cooper keep
you in after all this?

See you soon (hopefully),
alison

- -

PERCEIVED DISCIPLINARY ACCUSATION #5:

Interfering with several public servants in their duty, filing false reports, disturbing the public, provoking a riot, costing the community $50,000 in emergency response costs, and a few other charges my counsel has advised me not to discuss.

ACTUAL EVENT:

Trying to accurately prepare our school and community for an actual, real-world emergency (and as far as that $50,000, I'd like to see the figures they used to come up with that amount).

- -

Mr. Cooper, I know this perceived offense has caused you a lot of trouble, but at least you got to be on TV, right? Granted, maybe not for the reason you would have preferred, but being on the news is pretty cool nonetheless. (And you can admit it—you recorded it, didn't you? It's something to impress the relatives with at the next family reunion.)

But again, if you let me explain, you'll see all the trouble you've had to go through will actually be beneficial in the long run. My demonstration of the problems with your emergency-management system may result in the changes needed to save lives in the future. Maybe even cause a wing of the school to be renamed the Thaddeus A. Ledbetter Memorial Wing. Though let me check and see if that memorial designation means I have to be dead.

We may need to rethink the wing-naming. I'll get back to you, and this time, I think it would need to be a plaque and not one of your cheap certificates.

WELCOME TO THE

THADDEUS A. LEDBETTER MEMORIAL

COMPUTER, SCIENCE & ETYMOLOGY WING OF CROOKED CREEK MIDDLE SCHOOL.

(SO NAMED BECAUSE HE DID A REALLY COOL THING, NOT BECAUSE HE'S DEAD. HE'S ACTUALLY DOING QUITE WELL, THANK YOU VERY MUCH.)

The point being, yes, you may still be a bit perturbed, but when I explain it to you and you have time to calm down (have you seen a doctor recently? Your blood pressure must be through the roof with the way you overreact to every little thing) and put everything in perspective, you'll be glad I did what I did.

Like the old saying goes, you have to break some eggs to get an omelet—or at least an edible one.

THADDEUS A. LEDBETTER
DEFENSE

Let's go back to the beginning, to the main reason I've been placed in ISS and have had to work on my defense. Do you remember when we had that fire drill during the first week of school? (Which I suspect was planned so that you could meet the state-mandated number of minimum fire drills before the kids started acting up. I get it. It's easier to keep the kids under control when they're still scared of the teachers. This by itself indicates you're not taking disaster preparation as seriously as you should.)

Well, Mr. Cooper, your little fire drill could not have prepared us less for an actual disaster. If anything, it probably gave you a false sense of security that you are protecting your student body.

This couldn't be further from the truth. Life is too dangerous to be wasting time on useless drills.

> ### A Thaddeus Fun Fact
>
> "Drill," as in "fire drill," comes from the Germanic *threljanan*, which is not just a series of unrelated letters strung together that have nothing to do with those in the word "drill," as it first appears. My theory is that German is kind of a mumbly language that is easily misheard, so it changes a lot over time. Either way, it means "to practice military activities." What this has to do with screaming kids practicing running out of a burning building is beyond me. Maybe you should call in the military.

First of all, have you ever been around people when an actual emergency happens? Kids especially? Well, to be blunt, they freak out in the most illogical, unhelpful way possible. If anything, they make their situation worse. I know from experience.

See, one time at Scout camp, we were in the Hiawatha Mess Hall for dinner when a bat flew in. Somebody screamed, "Bat!" then "Rabies!" and then pandemonium ensued. Kids were climbing over tables, pushing one another down. I saw Alex Hurley push Justin Goertz right into a big vat of macaroni and cheese and not even stop to laugh. Why were the kids acting so out of character? Just because a flying mammal had mistakenly flown into the room. Even Scout Leader Hardy was screaming in this really high-pitched voice that, in all honesty, made me uncomfortable. You really don't want a leader of future men to sound like a little girl frightened by a mouse.

DEFENSE

Granted, the timing was perfect for such a response, since the night before, Scout Leader Hardy's ghost story was about a Scout who years ago had been bitten by a rabid chipmunk, gone nuts, and attacked the bread delivery man in a bloody scene of whole-wheat chaos. So everyone was a bit rabies-jumpy that night.

Still, these are trained woodsmen, or at least *woodskids*, and they did not respond in a calm, mannerly fashion to a perceived emergency. Shoot, we even have a whole chapter on how to handle emergencies in our Scout manual, and this still didn't help. (By the way, that whole "cut an X and suck out the poison" for snakebites is an urban myth. This is a bad idea on so many levels.)

Secondly, your drill comes under the assumption that disasters follow some sort of schedule, preferably a schedule of your convenience. No, an emergency is an emergency because you don't know it's going to happen. I can tell you from personal experience. Being unprepared for bad stuff is the worst thing a person has to deal with.

MR. FIRE'S TO-DO LIST FOR THURSDAY

- PICK UP DRY CLEANING
- TAKE CAT TO VET FOR WORM SHOT
- BUY SOME AA BATTERIES
- WRITE THANK-YOU NOTE TO KID WHO PLAYED WITH MATCHES
- 3:00 P.M. SHARP, START UP AND SPREAD QUICKLY AT CROOKED CREEK MIDDLE SCHOOL

We, the undersigned and students of Crooked Creek Middle School, believe and demand that Thaddeus Ledbetter, even though he is incredibly annoying, should be let out of ISS.

James Roe

Theodore Manson

Toni Elizabeth Bolyn

Jenny May Kinsey

Phoebe Halliwell

Mary Smithson

BLITH ALBERT

Emily Patterson

Leonard Nelson

Todd Hansen

Henry Applecott

MIKE HRANICA

Chrissy Simmons

BROOK HARDY

Tanner Catherson

Sabrina Gonzales

Tray Marvell

Katherine Howard

Alison Baker :)

Jane Seymore

Leanna Band

Amy Goldsmith

CLARK WALTON

Kurt Brewsky

Mrs. Garza

DEFENSE

Again, with all due respect, what exactly do they teach you in principal school? Your gross misunderstanding of basic human nature and your thinking that disasters are nice, organized events like a Veteran's Day assembly is disturbing. (By the way, I've got some good ideas on how to make the kids pay more attention to those old guys in the uniforms. Do we have any money in the assembly budget for live ammunition?)

No, if we are going to be prepared for a real emergency, we must know how to react to the unexpected. And by "we" I mean you, the teachers, and the kids. I'm excluding present company (that would be me) from the above statement because I've studied such situations closely and know what to do.

So I noticed something when I was waiting in your office to discuss my "Students Grade the Teachers" plan, and not to beat a dead horse, but this is another item I've brought to your attention that you have failed to address. What is it you do all day? Are you taking two-hour lunches or something? Your secretary must be covering for you, since every time I try to meet with you, you're in a "meeting." Sure.

A Thaddeus Fun Fact

The phrase "beat a dead horse" reflects some of the more unseemly aspects of our forefathers. Since this is pointing out the pointlessness of beating a dead horse, beating a live one must have been acceptable. I'm sure the ASPCA was not happy about this. And having to be told not to beat a dead horse leads me to believe our forefathers weren't real bright.

DEFENSE

Anyway, after I had let myself into your office when Mrs. Thomas had gone for coffee or some other personal errand that took her away from her assigned station, I couldn't help but notice that on your calendar you had scheduled a tornado drill for the following week. I saw this as what I believe you in the education business call a "teachable moment."

If we're going to have a drill to learn what to do in an emergency, let's do it right. Right? Let me ask you in the traditional way that kids pass notes in class.

Do you want to actually prepare the staff and student body for emergencies?

☐ Yes

☐ No

☐ Maybe (which seems to be your favorite answer)

OK, let me take you through my thought process. You had scheduled a tornado drill, or one in which we were to stay in our rooms and get away from the windows. Wow, a disaster in which we're supposed to just sit there. That's quite a drill. Maybe we can have a drill where all the kids remember to breathe. Or to have their hearts beat.

Do you see the problem here? Something needs to actually happen.

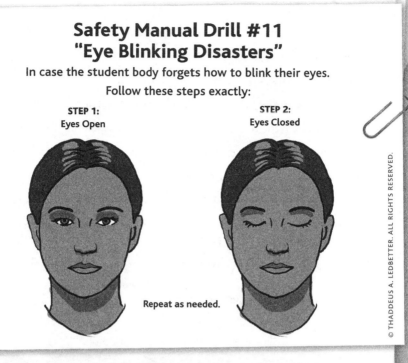

Safety Manual Drill #11
"Eye Blinking Disasters"

In case the student body forgets how to blink their eyes.
Follow these steps exactly:

STEP 1:
Eyes Open

STEP 2:
Eyes Closed

Repeat as needed.

I know you tell all the teachers in advance when we're having these drills, therefore their reactions are anything but natural. You're going to tell me that Mrs. Dixon is going to calmly pick up her grade book and purse during an emergency when she shrieks for ten minutes if she sees a spider? No, it was time to see what would happen if we really did need her, and the other teachers, to keep their heads on straight.

And since this was supposed to be real-world preparation for real-world disasters, as opposed to all of this meaningless nonsense in the curriculum (I know that was a little harsh, but it needed to be said), I did a little research into the biggest threats to kids our age.

THADDEUS A. LEDBETTER
DEFENSE

Do you know what the leading cause of death is for young teens (ages ten to fourteen)? Automobile accidents. This is interesting since KIDS DON'T DRIVE!!!!

So let's do the math. Kids don't drive cars + adults do = car wrecks are the number one killer of kids. Speaking for my generation, I would like to thank you adults for wiping out your children. That inspires a lot of confidence. Maybe they should drop the driving age to ten. It's not like we could do much worse.

Crooked Creek
MIDDLE SCHOOL

Thaddeus,

According to Mr. Cooper, you were responsible for the change in lesson plans. Well done!

At lunch today, Mrs. Dixon, Ms. Jimenez, and I were discussing how much more time we were actually teaching now instead of filling out forms, and how much better it was for us and the students.

There was even some talk about how having you and your "suggestions" in our classes was starting to be missed. Though, Mrs. Dixon was clear that she really didn't need any suggestions.

Just wanted to thank you,
Mrs. Garza

P.S. Still need to check your notebook.

Thaddeus,

You'll never guess what happened in Mrs. Dixon's class today! You know how I told you some of the kids had made "Free Thaddeus" shirts? Well, it really caught on. Even some kids in other classes who don't even know you have started wearing them (yes, I know you find it hard to believe, but not everyone knows you).

Anyway, a couple of kids were wearing them in Mrs. Dixon's class and she told them they were out of dress code. They wanted to know why, and she said they were "disrupting the learning process." Travis Trent said they weren't disrupting anything, and no one learned anything in her class anyway.

Well, she went off, turning all red and making those weird choking noises like she would do when you would call her on something, and then she tried to kick all the kids wearing your shirt out of class. Jake Black then told her that she didn't like the shirts because she didn't like you telling her how to do her job better, and that she had gotten to be an even worse teacher since you had been put in ISS. (over)

And then Billy told her to go eat a sandwich
(no one is sure why he said that or even what
it means, but it was funny).

I really thought she was going to have
a heart attack. All the kids then started
chanting "Thad-de-us Thad-de-us" and banging
their desks in rhythm. It was just like a
movie66

Then Mr. Cooper came in and calmed everyone
down. Mrs. Dixon went home and we had a sub
the rest of class. You would have loved it.

My mom thanks you for the note explaining
how to program her new answering machine.
She says she doesn't remember asking for your
help, but maybe you tried to call and got the
generic answering message. She says that this
is a good sign that you're getting back to your
old self.

Missing you,
Alison

DEFENSE

Due to the fact that getting run over by cars is the second deadliest threat to kids, we really should rename automobiles "Kid-Killing Machines." Seriously, is the primary objective of the automobile to transport people in a more efficient way or to negate the results of all those inoculations for childhood diseases by hitting young people with cars?

Just wondering. (If this is a strange adult conspiracy, while incredibly creepy, I will keep it a secret. I swear. Please don't kill me if I have stumbled upon some evil plan.)

Now, most folks probably think that a school would be a relatively safe place for kids when it comes to cars. There's not a lot of automotive traffic in our hallways, giving another reason why my important-student lane makes so much sense. But from my demonstration, you must now realize that is not the case. Sure, it might take a series of incredible coincidences to make car danger in a school possible, but it could happen, so we ought to prepare for it.

I got the idea when Sarah MacIntire's grandfather changed medications and passed out in the after-school pickup line with the car in drive. He leaned against the steering wheel and then drove in a circle for half an hour until he ran out of gas. That was cool. Though I still say Officer Hernandez should have shot the tires out. But it did get the kids' attention, especially James Roe. His bike got run over.

But for our purposes, car emergencies make the most sense to prepare for. Besides car accidents, most of the things that kids need to worry about really can't be prepared for: cancer, heart disease, congenital anomalies. For the complete list, please see thaddeus-ledbetter.com.

A Thaddeus Etymological Fun Fact

"Congenital" comes from the Latin *con,* meaning "at," and *gignere,* "to give birth"—putting it all together to mean "something that has already happened before you're born."

"Anomaly" comes from the Greek *anomalia,* meaning "uneven, irregular." In other words, a congenital anomaly means you were born with something that deviates from the usual human. Granted, most of the time it's not good and will kill you. Whatever the case, you can blame your parents. "Hey, Mom, thanks for the faulty DNA. Now I have a tail, and not one of those cool prehensile ones that I can pick stuff up with; just this one that lays there and makes it hard to buy pants."

My dad once asked my mom if she drank while pregnant (I must admit, I do seem to have superhuman insights sometimes. Maybe I'm a mutant!!), but she hit him with a dishtowel and told him to stop talking nonsense and come up with a plan to get the laundry done.

He's sad because his tail doesn't do anything. Impossible to buy jeans with premade "tail" hole.

tail

THADDEUS A. LEDBETTER
DEFENSE

Of course, I had to include the ol' school-drill mainstay, the fire drill. It's interesting. I can't find any reports of kids being hurt in school fires (though fires are #11 on the deadly list, they don't seem to happen at school). You'll probably credit good administration and yearly fire drills for this fact. I'm thinking it's new, noncombustible building materials.

And you already had the tornado drill planned, so that would be our jumping-off point.

We just needed one more element to make my scenario a true test of our disaster preparation: an attack of killer bees. Granted, there haven't been any reports of killer bees in our area, but you never know. A strange wind current picks up some bees, carries them a couple thousand miles, and plops down a giant swarm of very angry killer bees on our playground. Then what?

I thought of this the last time I was at the snow-cone stand with Alison. One little regular bee, maybe a bit grouchy, but by no means a killer, came near Alison's snow cone, and she went absolutely crazy. She started screaming and running around the picnic table.

I don't think the bee ever even touched her, but after all her screaming and running, the guy at the snow-cone stand made us leave. He said we were scaring the other customers.

I told him it wasn't us, but his bee problem that was causing the commotion. And what was the deal with the ants? Had he ever heard of an exterminator? And what kind of snow cone flavor is "Tiger Blood"? There was no blood or any tiger product involved. And what kind of sicko would want blood on a snow cone? Then I jotted down a list of other problems with his business plan and how to correct them (see attached).

How to Improve the Snow Cone Industry

Lose the "Tiger Blood" flavor. We're kids, not vampires. Plus, do you really want to encourage the slaughter of an endangered species as a kids' snack?

No Piña Colada and Margarita flavors. Getting the kids hooked on the flavors of alcoholic drinks isn't very responsible.

No naming flavors after popular cartoon characters. What does that mean? How are we supposed to know what fictional characters taste like? And why would we want to eat one?

Increase knowledge of food in the natural world. Like the flavor "Blue Coconut." Have you ever seen a coconut? They could not be less blue. If anything, that color would indicate spoilage, or at least some fungi growth. Either way, it isn't very appetizing.

Spend more on pest control.

THADDEUS A. LEDBETTER
DEFENSE

I was providing my services for free, yet this guy still acted like I was ruining his business. Next summer, my banishment from that snow-cone stand is over.

I should note that I may be allergic to bees like Robin Mitchell is. I have never been stung by a bee, though several have given me the eye when I wear my yellow shirt. But I still carry antihistamine in my emergency-preparation kit ever since I saw Robin drink that soda that a bee had flown into, and then his face swelled up like a basketball almost instantly. That's not a good look for anyone.

DEFENSE

Now, all of our previous encounters just dealt with a bee or two who seemed to just be in the neighborhood. What if it were millions of murderous bees with anger in their hearts? I thought we might as well get everyone's attention, especially Robin's, and adding the twist of bees looking for trouble into the drill would give us all the elements we needed to truly test our preparation level.

X number of students
÷ unprepared, easily upset teachers
= Accurate Determination of School Disaster Preparation

Doesn't the fact that I have mathematically proven the accuracy of my drill come into your decision-making process? You can use your calculator if you need help with the math.

THADDEUS A. LEDBETTER
DEFENSE

You've probably noticed that with so many moving parts, this demonstration was going to take a lot of planning and logistical prowess. Luckily, I was just the kid to do it. With less than a week to get everything organized, I had to get busy. I think you'll be impressed with the preparations, even if a bit perturbed at the results.

Let's big-picture this drill. What would happen if a fire started with a tornado approaching, and some old people were so distracted by the tornado that they crashed their cars into the school, with their crash disturbing a gigantic hive of killer bees that had just recently arrived from South America and were in a foul mood from the insect version of jet lag? That, Mr. Cooper, is what we found out, didn't we? I don't know about you, but I wasn't happy with our results. I think it's evident we have a lot of preparation to do in our preparation.

Since you were in charge of the tornado drill, that really didn't take any pre-drill preparation on my part. For the rest of the preparations, I made good use of my environmental group's recycling drive. Being the president and founder of the "Friends of the Planet" chapter at Crooked Creek Middle School, I recruited a few of my classmates to assist in the drill, namely James Roe, who was still mad about his bike being run over, and Billy Cunningham, who just likes excitement and figured there would be an opportunity to punch someone.

DEFENSE

Then I spent a couple of days telling Mr. Wardell, my science teacher, that I was really interested in killer bees. Granted, this was an obvious ploy, since I'm obviously a better expert on the insect world than anyone in the tristate area, but teachers always get all excited if you act the least bit interested in their subjects.

It's kind of cute. Since most of their lessons put students to sleep, if a teacher thinks you want to learn something from their usually useless curriculum, they go bananas. I mentioned a couple of times I was interested in killer, or "Africanized," bees, and Mr. Wardell spent the next three days showing us videos and doing worksheets about the spread and danger of killer bees.

Perfect. The kids had killer bees on their minds and were even a little jumpy when they saw a regular bee. This would add to the efficiency of my drill.

With all of the elements in place, the plan was this: On the day of the drill, we members of "Friends of the Planet" would be out on a "recycling run," picking up paper from all of the classrooms, and there is always a ton of paper to pick up since most teachers just pass out worksheets and then play on the Internet for the remainder of the class. (Again, a truth about your school that just had to be said.)

This way, we could be out in the halls at the perfect time to get my drill proceedings started and, more important, record the results to present to you and your emergency-management team afterward.

Please note that this was not just an exercise to point out your systems' weaknesses, but one to educate you and the school on how to improvise disaster preparation. My dad always said not to point out a problem unless you have a solution. Luckily, I have all kinds of solutions.

(Note: on the advice of my counsel, I am not admitting to anything. But I've read the law, and know it's illegal to cause a "false alarm," but since this happened while carrying out the duties of True Emergency Drill Coordinator, it's not technically "false."

Actually, my counsel [my uncle Pete—I believe you've heard from him] says I should just stop commenting on anything. He's always saying crazy stuff like that.)

THADDEUS A. LEDBETTER
DEFENSE

Now how to get some old people and their cars at the school, or preferably IN the school? Then it hit me. The classic-car club. I'd invite them to do a presentation. Those guys think everyone wants to see those old cars.

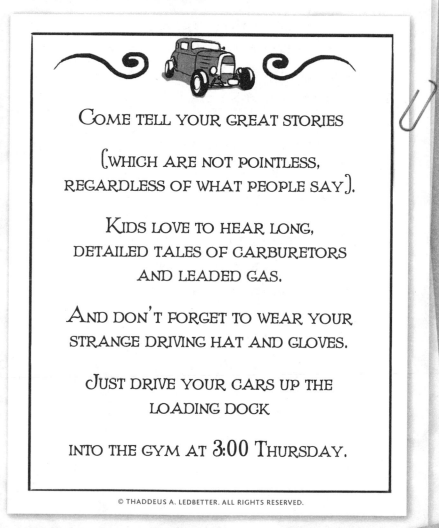

COME TELL YOUR GREAT STORIES

(WHICH ARE NOT POINTLESS, REGARDLESS OF WHAT PEOPLE SAY).

KIDS LOVE TO HEAR LONG, DETAILED TALES OF CARBURETORS AND LEADED GAS.

AND DON'T FORGET TO WEAR YOUR STRANGE DRIVING HAT AND GLOVES.

JUST DRIVE YOUR CARS UP THE LOADING DOCK

INTO THE GYM AT 3:00 THURSDAY.

Oldies but Goodies Car Club

Dear Mr. Ledbetter,

The members of the "Oldies but Goodies Car Club" would be happy to show our classic cars to your student body. We're always excited when the younger generation shows interest in these American classics.

We will arrive a little before 3:00. Isn't there a parking lot in which we could display our cars? It would be much easier.

If we really need to drive them inside, I guess we can, but please make sure there is plenty of room on both sides for us to enter. The members are very particular about their cars, especially their paint jobs, and we definitely don't want a scratched car.

Thanks for your interest and concern,

Frank Butterman
President of the Oldies but Goodies Car Club

Hey, Buttface

I see you're real popular these days. It's become cool to wear a "Free Thaddeus" T-shirt.

Well, guess what: I'm still going to kill you!!!!

I've been looking for you at the bus drop-off.

Where have you been hiding, you little weasel?

Billy the Executioner

Mr. Cooper, against advice, I have included my plans for the drill. I'm doing so to show you how carefully I designed this drill so that no one was in any real danger (excluding Mrs. Dixon, but, in my opinion, she really needs to lose some weight. She looks like she's on the verge of a heart attack just walking up the stairs, and her falling down and losing her wig could have happened anytime). Please keep these very mitigating circumstances in mind.

1 School's on "lockdown for tornado drill."

2 Classic cars enter the gymnasium.

Crooked Cree
MIDDLE SCHO

PLAYGROUND

COMPUTER LAB
C1

OFFICE

C2

C3

GIRL'S LOCKER

8 I had watched some videos on the Internet to get the right killer-bee pitch, so my tone was perfect.

124   123

121

TEACHER
PARKING LOT

BREAK
ROOM   FACULTY
LOUNGE

OFFICE

OFFICE

107   10

CLINIC

C   D

Of

7 Using the phone in the empty computer lab, all I had to do was punch in the code, announce, "Killer bees have infested the school! Take cover!" and then make a humming, buzzing noise over the intercom.

* 9 6

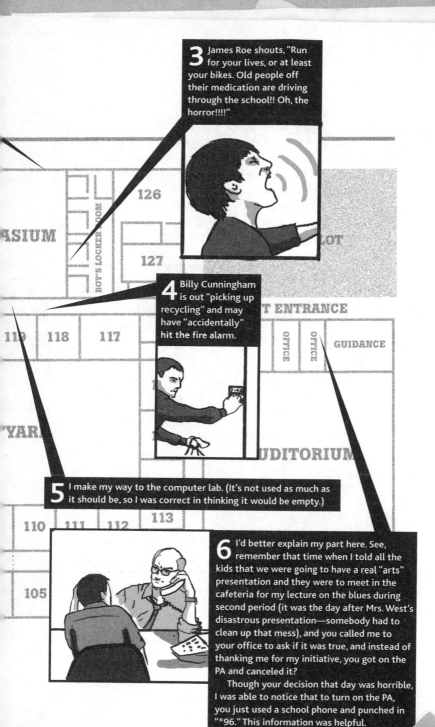

3 James Roe shouts, "Run for your lives, or at least your bikes. Old people off their medication are driving through the school!! Oh, the horror!!!!"

4 Billy Cunningham is out "picking up recycling" and may have "accidentally" hit the fire alarm.

5 I make my way to the computer lab. (It's not used as much as it should be, so I was correct in thinking it would be empty.)

6 I'd better explain my part here. See, remember that time when I told all the kids that we were going to have a real "arts" presentation and they were to meet in the cafeteria for my lecture on the blues during second period (it was the day after Mrs. West's disastrous presentation—somebody had to clean up that mess), and you called me to your office to ask if it was true, and instead of thanking me for my initiative, you got on the PA and canceled it?

Though your decision that day was horrible, I was able to notice that to turn on the PA, you just used a school phone and punched in "*96." This information was helpful.

DEFENSE

A Thaddeus Fun Fact

While most people have heard of the "fight or flight" instinctual choices humans make when faced with danger, it has been my observation that there is actually a third "F" choice: "Freak out!" I saw more people neither fighting nor flighting, but just standing there screaming in a very nonproductive way. Maybe the freak-out scared off the saber-toothed tiger when our forefathers did it, though I doubt it.

Here are the notes my team and I took during the drill. I was using a stopwatch, so the time increments are very exact. I can't say as much for my team, though.

Billy Cunningham's Report

Sorry, I couldn't find a pencil during the drill and my stopwatch kept resetting.

Who cares anyway? That was so cool! And if anyone asks, you don't know me and I was never near the fire alarm.

James Roe's Report

- 2:55 Car club members start arriving.
- 2:57 I start directing them into the gym.
- 3:00 Tornado drill starts. Car club members confused and a little scared.
- 3:01 Fire alarm goes off. Now car club members really confused, want to talk to someone in charge. Killer-bee buzzing starts and many members dive into their cars.
- 3:02 I start shouting, "Run for your lives and your bikes. Crazy old people driving into the school!" Car club members stare at me.
- 3:03 Car club president tells me to shut up.
- 3:04 Coach Michaels walks into gym and starts flipping out about cars being on gym floor.
- 3:05 Coach Michaels and car club president get into shoving match. I go hide behind bleachers and wait drill out.

Thaddeus A. Ledbetter's
(True Emergency Drill Coordinator) Official Report

- 2:45 – Excused from class to "supervise recycling paper pickup." (By the way, Ms. Jones is always very cooperative when I need to leave her class for my duties. You might want to put a note in her file about her good judgment.)

- 2:50 – Get Billy out of class to help me. Big surprise, but he had forgotten the plan, so good thing I was there to remind him.

- 2:52 – Get a very nervous James Roe out of class and send him to gym. (Note to self: James too jumpy for important projects.)

- 2:53 – The custodian, Mr. Wilson, was using the floor waxer incorrectly. Stop to give some pointers. Apparently can't hear me above the noise because he ignores me.

- 2:55 – Easily make my way into computer room and secure intercom. Lack of security around here is awful. Someone with bad intentions could cause a lot of trouble.

- 2:56 – Have a few minutes, so I update my blog by rating the day's nachos at lunch (B-. Cheese was a bit runny).

- 2:57 – Wait for tornado drill. Notice school defibrillator outside the computer lab. Can't open case. How am I supposed to practice? Make note to tell principal this.

- 2:58 – Call local radio station and report killer-bee attack at Crooked Creek. Promise to send weather guy over to cover story since the news guy is at court covering lawsuit of 12 families against nursing home for attempted negligent manslaughter. Sounds like a boring case.

- 3:00 – Hear tornado alarm go off. Maybe giggle a little bit.
- 3:01 – Hear fire alarm go off. Can't believe Billy got it right. Hope he remembers to take notes.
- 3:02 – Announce killer-bee alert over intercom. Make buzzing noise for two minutes. Add the occasional "Ouch!" or "They got me!"
- 3:05 – Hear James shouting about crazy old people driving cars into the school. He's not selling it as hard as he should. I hope people are believing it.
- 3:06 – Note drill results into my hand recorder to write later. Say "freaking out" 27 times and "no sense" 18 times.
- 3:07 – After recording data, I move out of command center to tell everyone to stand down, the drill is complete.
- 3:08 – As usual, no one is listening to me. Chaos continues. This school can't even handle the ending of a drill, let alone a real disaster.
- 3:10 – Help Mrs. Dixon up after she fell down for no apparent reason. Tried to help her put her wig back on, but this only made her madder. You just can't help some people.
- 3:12 – Kids are everywhere. No one seems to be in charge, kids are crying, and I hear sirens in the background. Wow, lots of sirens.

- 3:14 – Make my way to parking lot. According to my count, 7 police cars, 3 fire trucks, and several city pest-control vehicles are on scene. Don't see how mosquito spray trucks would help with killer bees, but still must commend them on their speedy deployment.
- 3:16 – Now everyone—police, firemen, pest control guys, teachers—are running around looking for something to do. Just seem to be running into one another and shouting.
- 3:17 – OK, I think I've made my point here. Time to stand down. I'll go explain the whole drill and debrief all those guys.
- 3:20 – Principal Cooper is pointing at me and shouting. Lots of folks rushing toward me. Need to . . .

A Parting Thaddeus Fun Fact

Archaeologists discovered that the Mayan calendar ends in 2012, and some people think this predicts the end of the world. Of course, it could have just been that the calendar maker thought, "This is like five hundred years from now. Why do I care?" and quit right there. But if the end-of-the-worlders are correct, do any of us want some great injustice we could have corrected hanging over us at the end of time? Just a thought.

DEFENSE

That's where my notes ended before my clipboard was rudely ripped from my hands. I was yanked into the office, and the angry shouting began. What's the deal with all the angry shouting? I understood immediately—no one was happy with my drill.

But still, our notes, mine at least, point out the many flaws in the current system, and I would not mind providing some improvements, even after all this time of being treated so unfairly. Of course, for me to make truly accurate suggestions, I must be taken out of In-School Suspension and placed back out among the general population.

By the way, why aren't James and Billy in suspension with me? I just thought about that. I'm not ratting them out or anything, and want you to know that I take full responsibility for and deserve all the credit for this drill. But no one even mentioned anyone else.

Still, this is feeling more and more like a personal vendetta against me. But I shall remain strong and committed to the welfare of the faculty and student body of Crooked Creek Middle School.

You must admit, that last statement was awfully big of me. Isn't it time we all acted like adults and let bygones be bygones? And not to get into your spiritual matters, but didn't I see you at church last Sunday? What was Pastor Snodgrass's sermon about? Something about forgiveness, maybe?

Looking forward to working with you soon,
Thaddeus A. Ledbetter (soon to be Esq.)

Thaddeus,

After several e-mails and phone calls, Mr. Cooper
has agreed to meet with me about your punishment. I
talked to your mom and she wants to come in to have
another opportunity to talk to Mr. Cooper. She also
got Pastor Snodgrass to agree to be there, too (he's
on your side now, right?).

The most important thing for you to do is stay out
of trouble and be on your best behavior until the
meeting. PLEASE promise me you will.

Uncle Pete

Subject: RE: Good News!

Sent: March 20

From: "Thaddeus Ledbetter" <thaddeus.ledbetter@ccms.edu>

To: Peter.Ledbetter@awlassociates.com

Uncle Pete,

I'm always on my best behavior.

Thaddeus

PRISON JOURNAL, CONTINUED

DAY 40:

- Got some great news from Uncle Pete today. He was able to schedule a meeting. Maybe Mr. Cooper will finally come to his senses and let me out.
- Started working on the explanation of the true emergency drill. Though it didn't work out quite as well as I would have liked, I still think it was a good drill that will help make us safer.
- This one is a little harder to defend because of legal ramifications. Have to be careful some sneaky lawyer can't twist my words.
- Mr. Cooper finally implemented one of my suggestions, and surprise, surprise: it worked! Even the teachers can finally see that good things happen when you implement my efficiency recommendations. I must be a chip off the ol' block.

DAY 41:

- Even after going through all my notes, this defense is tricky. Though I had to be careful, I was able to finish the defense today and send it to Mr. Cooper. Mrs. Calhoun swears she delivered it.
- Got news from Alison that the student body is finally voicing their concern about my absence and the negative impact it is having on the school.

- I sent an apology letter to the Car Club. That was the one thing I really did wrong during my drill. Sure, it helped make my point, but I can now see that to get those car guys all excited about kids seeing their cars wasn't cool. I made a note to myself to act like I was interested in their club and wave the next time I see them driving slowly down the road on a weekend.
- Still worried about Billy. He can really hold a grudge.

<u>3/21</u> Hesitantly agreed to have a meeting with Thaddeus, his mother, his uncle (and lawyer), and Pastor Snodgrass to discuss Thaddeus's punishment after many, many e-mails and phone calls from his uncle. For someone who wanted Thaddeus's head on a platter, Snodgrass sure changed his tune quickly. Apparently he doesn't just talk about forgiveness on Sundays, but expects everyone to live by the concept. Of course, it is a lot easier to be forgiving of Thaddeus when you just have to deal with him one day a week.

I will listen, but I will make my decision based on what is best for the school and for Thaddeus (and for me, for that matter).

<u>3/23</u> Because of Thaddeus's drill, I had to meet with the superintendent today. He wanted to make sure I was "qualified" to run my school. I tried to explain how this could have happened to any principal, but I found it impossible to communicate just what a challenge Thaddeus is. His actions have now put my job in jeopardy.

I'm postponing the meeting until I can think straight, but right now, I'm feeling his punishment is richly deserved.

<u>3/28</u> Can't put this off any longer. Hearing today.

DAY 42:

- Shirley sent me some cupcakes.
- Finished Dolly Madison report. Really made her come to life, if I do say so myself.
- Just got a note from the office. I'm supposed to report to Mr. Cooper's office at 12:30. That's about ten minutes from now. Maybe he's finally come to his senses and is going to let me out. Even better, maybe he really thought it through and is going to apologize, or even name a wing after me.
- Just got back from the meeting. Wow!! It was great!!! I think. When Mr. Cooper's secretary was walking me to his office, we had to go through the cafeteria, and it was right in the middle of lunch. At first, no one noticed, but then Brian Sassoon saw me and shouted, "It's Thaddeus!" and everyone turned and looked at me.
- Then a lot of the kids jumped up and started clapping and shouting, and the secretary tried to rush me through, but all these kids in "Free Thaddeus" shirts were blocking the way and chanting my name. (The shirts looked really amateurish. Make note to design a better one. I'm not sure anything gets done right around here when I'm not around.)
- But then Coach Goldstein and Coach Mixon (who are supposed to be on lunch duty, but instead were just gossiping and cutting in the lunch line) started pushing them out of the way so I could walk through.

- Hooray! They finally have installed my important-student lane, but goodness, that was a pretty heavy-handed enforcement of it with all that pushing and shoving. (Note: write up proposal for important-student lane without need for violence.)
- But we finally got through the lunchroom and down to Mr. Cooper's office. When I got there, my mom, Uncle Pete, and Pastor Snodgrass were all there waiting.
- I sat in the middle and congratulated everyone for finally coming to their senses. I knew the strain of my absence on the school, the church, and the community at large was having a detrimental effect.
- My mom told me to be quiet and just sit there.
- Then my mom explained to Mr. Cooper that she believed I had learned my lesson and would not be causing any more trouble. At this point, I was about to interject that I had not caused any actual trouble, rather had only improved various systems and procedures, so any trouble that I caused in the future would be the first, but, for some reason, decided against saying anything.
- Sometimes you have to let adults think they know what they are talking about. It helps their self-esteem.
- Pastor Snodgrass then told Mr. Cooper that if he could forgive me for setting him on fire (again, a gross misinterpretation of the facts), then couldn't Mr. Cooper also find it in his heart to forgive me?

- Finally, Uncle Pete said that he believed that my punishment was too extreme for the circumstances and he would be willing to pursue very expensive legal action against the school if necessary.
- The whole time, Mr. Cooper just sat there quietly listening, except for once saying it was now a "federal" case (not sure how that is relevant). Though I think I did see him crack a smile when I offered to do a workshop for the teachers on how a nonviolent important-student lane was also going to work for their benefit.
- Afterward, he said he would think seriously about my punishment, but would make no promises and would be contacting us about his official decision.
- Mom walked me back to ISS. She told me, for the most part, that she was proud of how I handled myself in the meeting, that I was becoming her little man, and that my dad would have been proud of me. . . . You know, I think he would be.

Dear Mrs. Rachel Ledbetter,

After long and careful consideration, much soul-searching, and speaking with the district's legal counsel, I have decided to place Thaddeus back into the regular population of Crooked Creek Middle School, thus ending his In-School Suspension early. Please understand that he is on EXTREME probation, and any discipline problems, regardless of his motivation, will revoke his standing and place him back in ISS.

While I now better understand Thaddeus and his motivation, I still have the entire school to think about and protect, so he will not be doing any more drills, authorized or not. I appreciate your help in this matter.

Sincerely,

Frank Cooper

Frank Cooper

April 7

Well, Mr. Cooper, I hope you are happy. I warned you, but you wouldn't listen. You just had to let Thaddeus out of ISS. In the week he has been back in my class, he has caused nothing but trouble. I have been careful to document every offense carefully while the children work on their worksheets. His offenses include:

- Pointing out when I put the decimal point in the wrong place while we were learning about percentages.
- Giving me a new map of the parking lot with my parking space in the VERY BACK corner, and then trying to tell me he did it for my benefit.
- Asking, in front of all the children, mind you, if we were going to be learning anything that might be useful in the real world. He tried to preface it with "all due respect," but it wasn't respectful at all.
- Rearranging my desk so that my grading process would be more efficient and timely. Apparently he doesn't think I grade quickly enough.
- Helping Billy Cunningham understand fractions by using an example of how many kids Billy has already punched versus how many kids are in the seventh grade. Should he be encouraging violence? I think not.
- Last but not least, he brought some "heart-healthy" diet tips he found on a Web site and "accidentally" left them on my desk, right next to the box of doughnuts I had brought as a special treat to myself for putting up with Thaddeus for a week.
- Do you see a pattern developing? Maybe the same pattern that got him in ISS in the first place? I sure do. You can use this as the documentation you need to put him back in.

Mrs. Dixon

Discipline Referral Form

Student's Name: <u>Thaddeus Ledbetter</u>   Grade: <u>7</u> Gender: <u>M</u>

Teacher's Name: _____

Mrs. Dixon,

I'll look into it, but these really aren't discipline issues. Let's give him a chance. And Jane, with all due respect, maybe you should listen to some of his suggestions.

Mr. Cooper

☐ Face-to-Face Conference with Parent

☐ Other _____

Action(s) Taken by Administrator

☐ Discussion   ☐ Verbal Reprimand

☐ Warning/Probation   ☐ Referred to Counselor

☐ Student Conference   ☐ Detention

☐ Contacted Parent   ☐ In-School Suspension (ISS)

☐ Detention   ☐ Expulsion

☐ D.A.E.P. Assignment   ☐ Referral to Law Enforcement

☐ Other _____

Administrator Signature <u>Principal Frank Cooper</u>
Student Signature <u>Thaddeus A. Ledbetter (soon to be Esq.)</u>